ON YOUR LEFT

ON YOUR LEFT

Jack Rightmyer

On Your Left
Copyright © 2025 by Jack Rightmyer

This is a work of fiction. Names, characters, places and incidents are the products of the author's imagination or are used fictitiously. Any resemblance to actual events, locales, or persons, living or dead, is entirely coincidental.

All rights reserved. No part of this book may be used or reproduced in any form, electronic or mechanical, including photocopying, recording, or scanning into any information storage and retrieval system, without written permission from the author except in the case of brief quotation embodied in critical articles and reviews.

Book design by Jessika Hazelton
Printed in the United States of America
The Troy Book Makers • Troy, New York • thetroybookmakers.com

To order additional copies of this title,
contact your favorite local bookstore
or visit www.shoptbmbooks.com

ISBN: 978-1-61468-962-1

DEDICATION

To all the wonderful athletes I've coached through the years. These are the kids in high school who are good students, never get in trouble and for fun they push themselves every afternoon from three to five pm to excel as athletes. These well-adjusted teenagers are not usually the main characters in novels, but even good kids can have worries and face hurdles in life.

"Looking back over a lifetime, you'll see that love was the answer to everything."
—Ray Bradbury

CHAPTER 1

I was supposed to be a basketball player. I was the tallest kid in my elementary class, and when I started playing the game in fourth grade my big play was to stand under the basketball rim and throw the ball up. If it missed, I'd get my own rebound and toss it up again till it went in. Not a lot of skill there, but I knew the object of the game, put the ball through the hoop. I did notice as I continued playing in grades five, six, seven and eight, that other players started to catch up to me in height and when that happened it was obvious I wasn't the star I used to pretend that I was.

It's not like I enjoyed basketball, but it's how I was known on the playground: "What's the weather like up there, Kevin?" I was often one of the first kids picked to play in any basketball pick-up game, so you can imagine my complete shock freshman year of high school, the morning after the tryouts, when I walked down to the coach's office to see the names of the fourteen players who made the team. My name wasn't there.

At first I thought these might be the names of the kids who were cut, but that wasn't right because the names of the best player's were on that sheet. For the first time in my life I was being sent the message that I didn't belong. I was one of the tallest kids on that court. I figured there had to be some sort of mistake. My eyes got a bit misty and suddenly I felt like everyone was staring at me, but then being so tall I often felt like everyone was staring at me.

"Kevin, I can't believe you didn't make the team," said someone to my right. I had no idea who it was. I just wanted to disappear. I thought I played okay at the tryout. All right, better than okay, but I guess these high-school coaches knew the truth. I really did suck at basketball.

But now I had to figure out who I was because I was no longer a basketball player. Was I going to be the high-school kid who rode to school on the bus every morning, disappeared in class, and then rode home unnoticed by anyone all day? I was never popular, but I was at least known as 'Kevin the basketball player.' I never really had any friends, but if there was a basketball game I was always included. I wasn't good at art. I couldn't play a musical instrument. I didn't even have a favorite band or singer. The day I got cut from the hoop team, it was like I was a stick figure on a chalkboard and I was suddenly erased. Now I was completely blank.

When my parents came home that night, they sat around the dinner table in a sort of angry silence as I told them how I had been cut from the team.

"Michael Jordan was cut from his high-school team," said my father getting up from the table. I wanted them to feel sorry for me or maybe even give me a hug or take me out for my favorite pizza. I didn't want a lecture.

"You're more than just a basketball player," said my mother, and then she turned to my father who was opening a bottle of beer. "Did you pick up my dress at the cleaners?"

"I knew I forgot something. I'll get it tomorrow on my way home."

"I know your job is important, but you need to help out more in this house. I can't do it all myself," and they began to argue back and forth like they seemed to do every night, and I just chewed my food in silence not tasting anything and just wishing I could disappear.

That night I decided to join the indoor track team. I heard a few kids talking about it in English class earlier that afternoon. One of the advantages of being quiet and sort of invisible is that you get to overhear a lot of things. "There are no cuts in track," said a short kid with bushy hair.

"Yeah, and I heard that everyone gets to be in the meet. Not like when I played soccer this fall and mostly just sat the bench," said another kid.

I was laying on my bed feeling sorry for myself, throwing a tennis ball up and down and trying to catch it with my eyes closed. If I joined the track team, I could stay away from this house and its anger every afternoon. I could just run and run till I collapsed. I could come home tired every night, and I could maybe meet some friends and maybe get invited over to their house and maybe even one of them would call me up on the phone or become a Facebook or Instagram friend.

Two days later I went to the Indoor Track Team Meeting, and here I am three years of running indoor track, outdoor track and cross country and I'm now known as 'Kevin the distance runner.' I was actually pretty good at running, and once I stopped growing and began to get more coordinated.

It's been a good thing to be a runner these last three years, but now that I'm seventeen and about to enter my senior year, well, it's about the only good thing in my life. My parents, who used to nit-pick back and forth for years, pretty much hate each other right now. When I was a freshman they used to argue about stupid things, but now they mostly don't talk to each other and around me they're all sorts of phony friendly. "Hi, Kevin, how was practice? How was school today?" It's all kind of robotic, and I'm pretty sure they never really hear anything I have to say. I hate it. You can taste the quiet in this house. It's so lonely most of the time. Maybe it would be better if I wasn't an only child. Maybe it would be better if I had some real friends at school. I still spend most of my time at home alone since I'm an only child. It's sort of pathetic when I watch a show on Netflix about kids my age who are out trying to score some booze on a Friday night, or talking to pretty girls at a party, while I'm home watching Doctor Who or old Olympic 1500-meter races on YouTube. I wouldn't know what to say to a girl. Sometimes I'm not even sure what to say to the guys on the team, and they don't usually talk to me. They like having me on a relay and they like having me on the cross country team because I'm a pretty fast runner now, but I don't think they like me. I'm not funny. I've got a lot of pimples on my face and the hair on my head grows in whatever direction it wants.

I'm not interested in drinking, but I wouldn't mind being asked to go out with the guys some night, mostly so I can get out of this house.

It's not as bad during the school year when I have stuff to do like homework, and after school practice, but in the summer I'm trapped right here in my suburban prison. So any chance I get, I put on my Nikes and go out for a run. Sometimes I have a route all mapped out, and sometimes I let my legs take me where they want to go. Some summer nights, while my parents sit around quietly arguing, saying nasty things back and forth or even worse just sitting there and not talking at all, I go out for a run to the lame local mall that should have closed down ten years ago and just walk around for an hour looking through books or video games, anything to avoid going home. I make sure to go to a mall where I know the track guys won't be. I go to the most lame mall in the world, the one where only people over age fifty buy stuff.

The lame mall is still better than being home on a summer night with my parents. It's that subtle nasty arguing they do that's the worst; the cold statements back and forth. "I thought I told you not to move my phone," my dad will say. "I don't like looking all over the house for it when it rings."

"And how many times have I told you not to leave it on the counter especially when I'm cooking," my mother will say.

My dad will give this cold psycho killer smile, "I need that phone. I get important calls from important people. I don't have time to look for it."

My mother will laugh. "We're so blessed to have such an important person living in our house." She'll then look over at me, "Aren't we, Kevin?" I really hate when they try to bring me into an argument on one side or the other, and they both do that.

If they could just yell and scream and blow off some of their anger, I know everyone would feel so much better. It's like they're an overheating car, smoking and sizzling and just about ready to explode. But they never do explode. They're just an overheated car sitting on the side of the road, never moving, never going forward.

The running helps me, because I can't stand still. I can't stay there. I have to let my anger drift away like my thoughts, taking me back to better memories…

…like years ago on our summer vacations in Maine or Cape Cod. We'd rent a cottage for a week, just the three or us, laughing in the cold Atlantic water, even in August, or playing card games at night, and always stopping out for a bucket of fried clams at Congdon's, our favorite place. But for the past four or five years, now that my dad works as a federal prosecutor, we don't go anywhere. My mom is a math teacher at a local high school, fortunately not mine, so she has time to get away.

"Kevin," she said to me at dinner during one of those freaking freezing days of February, "how would you like to bike from Lake Placid to Albany?"

It was a bit of a random question, and I shrugged as I forked up more spaghetti. As usual, dad was at the courthouse, putting in another late night in downtown Albany.

"It's one of those group bike rides. I've always wanted to do one," my mother continued. "It's only five days around July 4th. You bike about forty miles a day." As she talked she got more and more excited. "They hope to have three hundred other cyclists, and you tent every night. A truck moves your stuff from one location to the next."

"I'm not going to tent with you," I said, reaching for my glass of Gatorade, a drink I'd become addicted to since becoming a runner.

My mom smiled. "Okay, I'll buy you a single tent."

"Is Dad coming?"

My mother rolled her eyes. "He's invited, but the federal government, along with the Western Hemisphere, might just fall apart if he does."

I'm not such a big runner in July. It's usually so puke-hot and muggy. That's when I like to bike or swim. "I'll do the bike ride," I said, thinking she'd forget. It was five months away. There's no way she'd remember. But then I thought, maybe my Dad would want to come along. He's always been one of those outdoor kind of guys. Biking from Lake Placid to Albany with three hundred other people is the kind of thing he'd jump at. He's a pretty social guy when he's not home, and I could see him laughing it up every night by the tent and joking on the bike with a group of us every day. And he'd definitely come along if there was some judge doing it, but what were the odds of that? Well, if nothing else, if the three of us went on the trip, maybe my parents would start liking each other again, and when I came home from college next year they'd both be living in the same house and I wouldn't have to spend one night with my mother wherever she'd be living and one night with my dad in his apartment, and what would happen to the house I had grown up in? Would it be sold and would another family be living there? Who would be sleeping in the only bedroom I've ever known? And if my parents got divorced, would they be broke, and would I have to go to some junior college for a few years?

But she didn't forget. She's one of those types who get these great ideas but don't always follow up on them, and the more I thought about that ride with the two of them, the more I wanted to do it. It's not like I'd see anyone I knew on the ride.

My mom bought me a single-person tent, and she bought me two pairs of those skin-tight bike shorts. In the spring, she brought my bike, a Cannondale I've had for a few years, into a cycle shop and had new tires put on and had the guy fix up my gears and my brakes, and before I knew it, I was standing in the Rensselaer Train Station parking lot with my mom putting our bikes on a truck that would bring them over one hundred miles north to Lake Placid. We loaded our bags filled with our clothes, sleeping bags, and tents and placed them on another truck. The two of us were soon seated together on an air-conditioned charter bus. It was filled with mostly old people, who didn't look very fit to me. There was a lot of gray hair on that bus, but none of it belonged to my dad. For months my mom had tried to convince him, and at one time he was planning to go, but there was some big case coming up in July. "I can't get away for even a few days," he said a week before the trip.

"Think of how much fun you're going to miss biking on those hot days," I said flashing a smile. I really did want him to go. That was the main reason I was willing to do it.

"I wish I could. Really. It's killing me that I can't."

My mom just nodded her head. It was one of our infrequent dinners together. She had a sort of crooked smile on her face. "We need Italian dressing for the salad," she said, pointing to the refrigerator, and for the rest of the meal she refused to look at my father. Just another pleasant evening at the Walsh home.

As the charter bus headed north, I wondered why I had gotten myself into this mess. When my dad dropped out of the trip, I wanted to bail, but I couldn't leave my mother all alone. And now here I was trapped with my mom and these old people who were wearing their much too-tight shorts. Some of the old guys had white chest hair sticking out of their spandex bike shirts. And why were they wearing bike shirts and bike shorts on the bus anyway?

"This is so exciting, isn't it? Can you believe we're going to bike across a big part of New York State?" My mother wore a scary clown-face grin. She clearly needed to get out more often.

I just kept scrolling through my Twitter feed reading about my favorite distance runners. "Yeah, this is great."

For a while my mom tried to get a conversation going, and I tended to give her the shortest answers I could. I've never been much for talking. I suspect I might be on the spectrum of Aspergers, some type of ailment where you can't socialize. When I was a freshman and had just joined the track team I heard one of the older guys refer to me as that new Aspergers' kid. When I got home that afternoon I told my mom about that and asked her what it meant. She proceeded to give me an informal lesson where we looked it up on the internet, and I was worried I was going to have an exam on it. What I do remember is that the syndrome was named after some Austrian guy, a doctor I think ,who described children in his care who had basically no friends, couldn't understand the way other people felt, and most of them liked to do solitary things. "Clearly, you don't have it," said my mom. I smiled, nodded my head and thought, it sure sounds like I have it.

I felt like I was on a bus to old person's camp. There was a guy from Virginia sitting across the aisle from me. "Where ya' from, boy?" He had this strong Southern accent. All he needed was a harmonica, and I would have felt like I was in an old Civil War movie.

"Outside of Albany," I said, barely looking in his direction.

"And who is that sitting next to you?"

It's not the first time I heard stuff like that, and it always creeped me out. "That's my mother."

My mom looked away from her Oprah magazine and introduced herself. The Virginia guy was all excited about introducing himself and his wife next to him. He was even more excited to tell us all about the other bike trips he had done. He must have named a dozen places he'd been to just in Virginia, and half of them might have been Civil War battlefields, for all I knew. I just wanted to get back to the article on how to be a better hill runner, but with mom in one ear and him in the other, I couldn't concentrate. I put my head back, closed my eyes, and wished the bus could do some hyper speed to get us there immediately.

It took about two hours to get to Lake Placid. It was a ride I've taken maybe a hundred times, but I've never gotten sick of it. Years ago we were a big hiking family, and my dad always talked about how we were going to climb the "46"—the forty-six Adirondack peaks that are over 4,000 feet high. But we only got to fourteen or fifteen, and then the magic of hiking just seemed to die, or maybe it was the magic of doing something together. One day we were hiking mountains and going on vacations to the ocean and laughing at the dinner table, and the next day my parents just sort of hated each other, and my dad started to eat dinner in the office a lot and go away on business trips. There wasn't much laughing in the house anymore, and home was no longer a fun place to be. It sure helped my running, though.

Just when the boring conversations of all the people around me were about to make me smash my face against the window, we got off the exit for Lake Placid and turned down the narrow Route 73 through the little town of Keene. Most people on the bus, "the campers" as I thought of them, had finally stopped talking and were consumed with looking out the windows at the mountains and blue water streams and ponds, and that was the first time I felt a little scared thinking I would have to bike the whole way home. What if I couldn't do it? What if my butt started hurting so bad I didn't want to get on the bike for another ride? What if my mom could do it and I couldn't? Mom told a few of her friends about this, and I'm sure they told their kids. Some of them I knew, and they'd know if I didn't make it. If that happened, I'd never hear the end of it. I'd have to take another bike ride into the sunset and just disappear forever.

We went by that road you take when you climb Mt. Marcy. I never get tired of looking down that road, with the big meadow in front and the high peaks in the distance. It's like some picture from the Rocky Mountains, and everyone on the bus started making sighing sounds and pointing out the window. We drove by Mt. Van Hoevenberg where they had the Olympic cross-country ski events in 1980. I had a fun day there about five years ago with my parents skiing on the actual trails used in the Olympics. After we skied around for a few hours, we went over and watched people race down the bobsled track. They just flew by us at like a hundred miles an hour. It was one of the best days I ever had.

"I'm glad we don't have to bike these hills," I said to my mom.

"I don't think I could do it, in the Lake Placid Triathalon they actually bike through here," she said.

"That's freakin' crazy." Out of the corner of my eye, I saw the Virginia guy shake his head. I don't think he approved of my language.

The bus pulled into the parking lot of a school in Lake Placid. The school sat right on Main Street next to the Olympic figure-skating and ice-hockey arena. An Olympic flag flew next to the U.S. flag, causing just about everyone to reach for their phones to snap a few selfies. They all acted like we had just arrived at Disney World.

Cars and pedestrians crowded the town of Lake Placid. I always liked the look of this town with Whiteface Mountain looming high overhead, like it's staring at you, but I couldn't focus on any of it. Instead, I wondered what my dad was doing at that time. It would have been great to get off the bus and see him waiting there for us with his bike. "I changed my schedule," he'd say. "I want to do this ride with the two of you." When we left that morning he was on the phone with another attorney about some big drug arrest in Plattsburgh. He didn't even look up when we walked out the door. Not exactly a movie send-off.

"Here we are," said the guy from Virginia, standing up in the bus aisle and stretching his legs. The guy was old, but his legs looked strong. Call me weird, but as a runner, I notice these things. I figured if he's a runner, he couldn't be all bad.

"There's tent city," said my mom, pointing out the window. Fifty or sixty tents, of all different sizes, shapes, and colors dotted the grounds of the high school. People rushed about placing sleeping bags and pillows inside them.

When I stepped down from the bus, I looked around quickly and saw no sign of my dad. What was I thinking? His job was too important to take a week off and bike with us.

"This is so exciting," said my mom, with that forced clown smile.

CHAPTER 2

The first thing we did when we got off the bus was find the truck that had our gear. We had to wait in line for a few minutes, and it suddenly occurred to me that I was going to be spending a lot of time this week in lines—lines for breakfast, lines for dinner, lines to use the bathroom. I hate lines.

It was two o'clock in the afternoon, and I stood directly in the hot sun, dripping sweat like I was coming around the final turn in the 3200-meter run. The big guy standing in front of me wore a sweat-stained, bright-orange, blue, and red bike shirt tucked into black bike shorts. Some people should never be allowed to wear spandex. Parts of him bulged out everywhere.

Once we finally got our bags, I followed my mom to the field in front of the school where most of the tents were set up. As we stepped over a cement track encircling the field where all the tents were, I remembered my dad telling me that at the 1980 Winter Olympics they flooded this and froze it for the speed-skating events, and a guy named Eric Heiden won something like five gold medals. "Hey, what are those over there?" I nodded toward row upon row of big tents to our left. It looked like the place where the generals lived while preparing strategy for the Battle of Gettysburg.

"Those must be the comfy campers," said my mom.

"What are comfy campers?"

"This is a good spot." My mom dropped her bag in the middle of the green field. We were on some thick, plush grass, with a great view of the mountains all around us. "For some extra money, we could have someone put up a tent every day. Those are the comfy campers, but I think the true experience is the way we're doing it."

I could see workers carrying big air mattresses to the comfy campers and putting them inside the enormous tents. "I wouldn't mind being one of the comfy campers," I said. "I'd love to sleep on one of those air mattresses."

My mom was already spreading out her tent, as if she couldn't wait to sleep on the ground. She pulled out her poles that were collapsed like some giant spider and began to fit them together. She really knew what she was doing. "Here, help me with this," she said, and I helped her fit the poles into the tent slots. I had done this a couple of times on our few family camping trips, but it always seemed very confusing to me. My mom was patient as she told me everything to do. How did she get so good at this?

Her tent now up, she tried to figure out where the wind was coming from so she could open the tent flap in that direction. "You want to get a breeze in the tent. It'll keep it cool."

There wasn't much of a breeze, and sweat now dripped off my forehead. Even my back was sweaty. Wasn't Lake Placid supposed to be one of the coldest places in New York State?

My mom blew into her small sleeping mat, placing it, along with her sleeping bag, inside her tent. It sure didn't look as comfy as those big air mattresses, but she didn't seem to mind. In fact, she looked as if she couldn't wait to lay down on it and get a good night's sleep before our big ride tomorrow. She placed her bag of clothes and her pillow inside, zipped up the tent, and said, "Now it's your turn."

A few months earlier, when she first bought it for me, we set it up together in our basement. It was no problem then, but now I just stood there in a panic looking at the pile of tent and poles and spikes that had fallen out of the bag. My mom sat down next to me. "You just helped me set up my tent. Think about how you should start."

There were other people around me setting up their own tents, and I was suddenly embarrassed that I didn't know what to do. I tried to remember how my mom began, and whenever I'd attach something my mom would offer encouragement like, "That's it," or "Think about what you need to do next." I also reached for plenty of the wrong things and my mom often said "Nope, not that. It doesn't go there." It took me twice as long to put up my little single tent as it took her to set up her three-person tent, but after making many wrong moves, she finally cheered and clapped her hands to congratulate me, which embarrassed me more than the sweat stains spreading on my shirt. I also felt like everyone in the town was watching me, and I hate when people notice me.

"In a few days, you'll have that tent set up and taken down faster than anyone here." She gave me a big grin.

I shrugged and continued to place my flimsy sleeping pad and sleeping bag inside my little tent. The sleeping bag barely fit inside the tent, and I looked longingly over at the comfy campers who were all sitting in little beach chairs beside their enormous tents. My single-person tent could fit comfortably inside one of their comfy tents. "I don't think my clothes will fit inside this tent," I said, trying not to whine.

My mom disappeared into her tent, rummaging through her bag for something. "You can keep your clothes bag in here at night," she said before emerging from her tent. "Now, let's get our bikes and go register."

Our bikes were stacked next to about fifty others beside a truck. We found them quickly and brought them over to our tents where we rested them together and wrapped our bike lock around them. We were both so hot that we hoped the registration desk would be inside an air-conditioned building. but it wasn't. It was inside the school's athletic fieldhouse. The place was muggy, damp, and the air seemed like something you'd find in an old crypt. We had to wait in line for maybe fifteen minutes which meant we had to have that phony chatter with everyone in front and behind us. "Very hot. Might rain tonight. Gonna be hot tomorrow. Hot all week is what I heard." I hate long lines.

When we finally got to the front of the table and signed in we had to fill out our names on a license-plate-looking thing that we had to place on the back of our bikes. I wanted to just write "Kick Me" but my mom said it would be inappropriate, which it would be, but it would also be funny. We were given a general schedule for the week about how far we'd bike each day and some places we could stop and visit. They even suggested we join a short bike ride to the John Brown Farm in an hour or so, but neither of us wanted to go on any ride at that moment. John Brown was an abolitionist guy who led a raid on Harper's Ferry hoping to end slavery. Apparently, he lived not too far from Lake Placid. After the lady at the registration table gave us each a shirt and a water bottle, my mom said, "I can't stand how hot it is. I need to take a shower."

I've never been too big about taking a shower with a bunch of naked people. I've had to do it a few times for long-away track or cross-country meets, but mostly I avoid it whenever I can. "I think I'll shower after tomorrow's ride," I said.

"They have these big shower trucks," said my mom, pointing toward one in the school's parking lot. A few people walked over there with towels. "I did pay extra to get us a clean towel every day."

"Wow! Thanks for splurging on that," I said, glancing back again at the comfy campers. I hope I didn't sound sarcastic, but I'm sure I did. I'm seventeen. I can't help it. It comes naturally.

My mom pointed to a big tent just beyond the comfy campers. "I bet that's where you get the clean towels."

How did she ever get to know all this stuff? She must have really done her homework before this trip. It figures—she's a math teacher. "Maybe I'll walk over to Mirror Lake, sit on a bench, and try to find some shade." I really just wanted to get away from all these excited biker people, play on my phone and maybe look through the biking pamphlet they gave us.

My mom was now on her knees with her head in the tent looking through her clothes bag to find something clean.

She exited her tent holding some brightly colored clothes, shorts, and a tank top. "I won't be too long," she said.

I nodded. "Should I stay by the tents?" I figured I could use my phone here, even if it would be a bit cooler by the lake.

My mom shook her head. "No, but when you leave, make sure your tent is zipped up so bugs don't get in. I'll walk over and look for you when I'm done. Don't leave anything valuable here." And then she waved and walked away to get her towel.

I took my bike pack that held my new water bottle, my wallet, and my cell phone and headed toward Main Street. The sun was blistering hot, and it was nice to cross the street and find some shady trees on my way to the lake. Mirror Lake is a pretty blue body of water in the middle of this cute Adirondack town. I found a bench in the shade at the end of one of the beaches and sat down. Several little kids splashed around, with their moms watching their every move. I didn't need the water. I was just happy to get cell phone reception where I could check out what was going on in the world and look through my messages. Like most teenagers my age, I'm pretty much addicted to my phone. It kind of relieves my boredom.

I had a few messages, but not the one I wanted. Not one from my dad.

Two sort of runner friends, Dwight and Patrick, were asking the top runners to meet for a long run on Sunday, and my friend, Dipper, wanted to know if I wanted to see some zombie flick that just opened. I wrote back reminding him I wouldn't be around this weekend. Dipper is a great guy, nice and all, and really my only true friend, but he's sort of clueless. He doesn't pay attention much when you tell him things. I know I'm not the most important person for any social event, and most of my so-called track friends have probably forgotten I was even doing this bike ride, but Dipper should know better. We first met when we came out for indoor track as scrawny freshman. Neither of us were popular so we latched on to each other. We're still not so popular.

I get invited to the long runs sometimes during the summer before cross country season, but I know I'd never get an invite if I wasn't one of the top runners on the team. Not too many of the guys talk to me, and I'm not the type to joke around much anyway. I always seem to think of the good, funny lines after everyone has left. There's one of those famous quotes that a writer is someone who thinks of all the funny lines on the way home from the party. Well, I'm one of those guys.

I checked my messages one more time. Still nothing from Dad.

I figure the only way he's going to write me is if I write him first.

WE GOT HERE OK. IT'S HOT. SET UP OUR TENTS. DINNER IN ABOUT TWO HOURS. WISH YOU WERE HERE.

I looked at that text for a few seconds, then decided to erase the WISH YOU WERE HERE. I hit SEND with a bit of hesitation.

There's no beep back. Nothing. Not for a minute; not for two. He probably doesn't even have his phone on him, or he's not paying attention to it. Either way, he's not writing me back. Not now. Maybe never.

I held my phone against my hand so I could feel it vibrate just in case.

I leaned back against the bench. It was nice and somewhat cool sitting there, a soft breeze blowing in from the lake. I played around with my cell phone, looking at a few things on the internet so I'd look busy and not like some homeless guy in the park. That's when a girl's voice asked me, "Is there a bathroom near here?"

I pointed to my left without really looking up, and then she asked, "Hey, aren't you Kevin Walsh?"

I was pretty shocked to hear my name, and I immediately looked up. She was an African-American girl, probably my age, wearing bright pink running shorts and she was wearing a Freihofer's Run for Women light green shirt.

"Yeah."

"It's the shirt you're wearing?"

I looked down and noticed I was wearing a cotton shirt with the name of my school and below that the word Cross Country.

"Are you doing the bike ride?" she asked. She flashed me a smile.

"Yeah." How did she know that? I put my phone down by my side wanting to ask who she was, but not so sure I should. I mean, what if I met her and was supposed to know her name?

"I figured you were biking when I saw your bike pack. I'm Taylor."

The two of us just looked at each other, and I wasn't sure if I was supposed to say anything or maybe wave, so instead I just kept looking at her.

"Taylor Lewis," the girl continued. "I run for Holy Family. I'm doing the bike ride with my grandfather. He's big into biking."

Holy Family had one of the best girls' cross country teams in the state.

"You're a great runner," she said. "I've seen you run lots of times. You're really fast. God, I hope that doesn't sound creepy. It's not like I'm stalking you or anything. I like to watch the top runners, and you're usually right there. You came in the top ten at sectionals last fall. That was amazing! I hope that someday I might be one of the top runners, too."

I was amazed that some girl had actually noticed me running, even if she did talk a lot. "Eighth. I was eighth at sectionals last year. You have a good team," I said sort of stumbling on each word. I didn't remember ever seeing her run.

"We have a chance to win states this fall; maybe even go to the Nike National Meet. Anyway, that's what we're hoping for. I'm glad you're doing this ride. Maybe we can bike together this week."

And then she gave me a quick wave and was off down the sidewalk in the direction of the bathroom. I sat there for a few seconds wondering if I should stay or leave. I wasn't sure what to say to her next. I've never been a smooth talker to girls my age, or really girls of any age. Before I left the bench, I checked my phone one more time. Nothing. No messages from anyone. Not even Dipper. I slipped my phone in my bike pack and began walking back toward the tent taking one last look in the direction of the girls bathroom.

When I got back, my mom was drying her hair with a white towel. "The truck showers are great," she said. It seemed lately like my mom thought everything was great. "They're warm, and they have great pressure. Are you hungry?"

"Yeah." My mom was wearing a tight black tank top. "There's a wine and cheese party that just started. It's over by the cafeteria."

"Sweet! Wine!" I smiled.

My mom smiled right back. "You can certainly have some cheese."

As we walked toward the cafeteria, I began to feel a bit nervous. I could hear some old guy strumming a guitar and singing and I could see people were standing around near him talking and laughing. A few people were singing along with him and moving to the music. I've never liked these big social parties. That's one reason why I like to run so much. It's quiet especially on those deserted back roads or trails deep in the woods. But now I was faced with what seemed like hundreds of adults standing around talking, holding a drink in one hand and shoveling crackers into their mouths with the other. It must be horrible being an adult and having to do that sort of thing. Do they do that every week? Most of the adults seemed to be staring at the two of us as we walked toward them. I could feel almost every eyeball on me.

"They have some iced tea over there," said my mom, pointing to a blue cooler. How did she know that? "I'm going to get a glass of wine. Meet me at that bench near the cafeteria in five minutes."

I nodded my head as my mom walked away. She seemed so relaxed, smiling at people at a nearby table and picking up a glass of white wine. She seemed so confident as she walked through the crowd. It's kind of the way girls acted around Dwight, our school's top runner. He walks down the hall and people just circle around him, particularly the girls. Dwight gets noticed even more than the football stars at my school, and that never happens to a distance runner.

I reached my hand in to get a plastic iced tea bottle. It was nice and cold. I held it up to my forehead, which cooled me off right away. I turned toward a nearby bench, while my mom put some cheese and crackers on a plate and joked with a grey-haired guy next to her. Seconds after I sat down on the bench, the dude playing the guitar got considerably louder because they set up a microphone by him. He was playing oldie's music—James Taylor, I think, or someone like that. Music this crowd would probably drool over. I knew my mom was loving it because she started swaying back and forth with a sort of far-away look. I haven't seen her move like that in a long time.

"They also had some cookies," said my mom, a few minutes later when she came and sat down next to me. She was followed by two guys about my mom's age. She moved the platter of cookies, crackers and cheese in my direction. I picked out a chocolate chip cookie.

"I'm shocked," said one of the older guys. He had a sort of French accent. "You said you were biking with your son, but I imagined him to be quite young. This is a man."

My mom laughed. "This is my son. Kevin, I'd like you to meet Jacques and Murray."

I nodded my head and continued to chew my cookie. How was she able to get their names in only a few minutes?

Jacques smiled at me. "You have such an adevnterous mom going on a bike trip like this."

I shrugged, and I think I stopped chewing my cookie. I didn't know what to say. It suddenly felt sort of awkward sitting there with the three of them watching me.

"Jacques and Murray are from Ottawa."

How did she know that? "Canada, huh?" I said, looking for a cracker and the perfect slice of cheese— one that wasn't too spicy or bitter.

"That it is," said Jacques. "Murray and I have done a few of these bike tours. Have you ever done one before?"

Jacques was talking to my mom now. I could tell he was more interested in her than he was in me. He even put his hand on her shoulder to brush away a fly or something. I chewed my cracker and wondered if this Murray guy could speak. He just stood around with a goofy smile.

After fifteen or twenty minutes, the guitar guy announced that food was being served in the dining hall. Jacques immediately extended his arm, gesturing my mother forward, making it perfectly clear he would be joining us for dinner. The four of us, with Murray bringing up the rear, waited in line for nearly ten minutes, Jacques asking my mother one question after another. It was like he was some sort of journalist, or maybe a lawyer like my father who could also fire off one question after another without ever taking a breath.

The pasta was that curly kind and it was quite good, but there was no air-conditioning, and all these bodies crowded together turned the place into an armpit-smelling oven. I found it difficult to breathe. Murray finally said something, but it took him all the way until dessert. "It's good vanilla ice cream," he said. A profound conversationalist, I thought.

My mom tried her best to get me into the conversation, but I mostly just sat and ate. There were all sorts of colorful flags from different countries hanging down from the ceiling. I felt like I was eating a meal at Hogwarts. I did look for Taylor but couldn't find her. The

Virginia guy and his wife came over. "You all enjoyin' yer' meal?" he asked. We nodded our approval.

After dinner, we gradually made our way to the auditorium where one speaker after another talked about the upcoming week of biking. "This is our first Adirondack Bike Tour, and we're going to make a few mistakes," said some dull bald guy named Al, who might have been the tour director. He was about as exciting as my calculus teacher. "This tour is not a race. There will be some elevation change every day, but nothing too significant. We've kept the daily mileage reasonable since we want you to take some time in the afternoons to see what our beautiful Adirondack towns have to offer." He mentioned some of the sights we'd see: Saranac Lake, Blue Mountain Lake, the Wild Center, Lake George, and the Saratoga Battlefield, but I wasn't really paying attention. There were many introductions, and too many rounds of polite applause. The loudest cheer of all was for the man who was the massage therapist.

There were something like 300 bikers from twelve different states and three countries. The oldest biker was 89 years old, and when they called his name he waved from the back of the auditorium. He was a short, wrinkly guy wearing a white biking cap and eating a banana. He didn't smile when he waved.

"Isn't that amazing?" my mom said. I think she may have had a tear in her eye.

When the talks were over, Murray and Jacques walked out of the building with us, giving advice on how to proceed the first day—what to do, what to wear, stuff we already knew. When we got outside we said goodbye to them and walked in the direction of our tents. Murray and Jacques had tents closer to the cement track, but I was hoping they might have been with the comfy campers. Somewhere far away from us.

"Looks like you made some friends already," I said.

"Oh, they seem pretty harmless," said my mom. "I'm tired. It's been a long day, but I'd love to take a quick walk through town with you. I love Lake Placid."

It's not a long stretch to walk from one end of Main Street to the other, and I did want to get away from tent city. Lake Placid is not your typical Adirondack town. It's very much a place for people who don't usually go to the mountains. There were a lot of stores that rich people would shop in. Most people from the Adirondacks like to shop in old general stores or hardware stores, but in Lake Placid we passed a bunch of restaurants, some of them were kind of fancy, a few bars, some jewelry stores that were closing up, a Starbucks, an EMS, a bookstore and a neat looking old movie theater. There were signs up in most of the stores 'Welcome Adirondack Bikers'. We didn't talk too much, but we did reminisce a bit about some of our other trips to town. "Do you remember when the three of us took the paddle boats on Mirror Lake?" I said.

My mom laughed. "That was some hard work, but we sure laughed a lot, didn't we?"

I wondered if we'd ever laugh like that again. At least as a family. I pointed to the full moon just climbing into the sky over the tree tops and said, "I'm sort of glad we're doing this." And at that moment, I was kind of ok to be doing this bike ride.

Even though it was pretty dark, I knew my mom was smiling.

When we got back to our tents, I told her I was going to brush my teeth in the school bathroom and charge up my cell phone.

"I'll walk over with you."

It was completely dark now when we walked over. It was mostly quiet in tent city. There were a few people talking quietly and clearing their throats, and I could hear some occasional zippers on tents going up and down. I carried a toothbrush, a half-used roll of toothpaste, and my cord to charge my cell phone, while my mom lugged two separate bags filled with all sorts of little bottles of creams and face wash and God knows what else.

"How do you feel about tomorrow?" she asked just above a whisper.

"A little nervous," I answered. "I always feel a little nervous before a race, and this feels a little like a race. A long race. I've never biked more than thirty miles, and I'm not sure I can do more than that for five straight days."

"You'll be fine. You've never dropped out of a race."

I laughed.

"Thanks for doing this."

I shrugged.

"Maybe next summer we can talk your father into spending a vacation with us."

"Maybe," I said, but I knew that next summer I'd be busy getting ready for college. Lately I had noticed my mother seemed pretty lonely, and if she was this lonely with me around, what would she be like next year when I was gone?

As usual, there was a line to use the bathroom. Fortunately, the men's room always takes less time. "See you in the morning," I said to my mom as I disappeared inside the men's room.

"Don't lose that mini-flashlight or you'll never find your tent—and remember, the alarm is going off at 6:00 a.m.," she said.

I groaned.

It was pretty quiet in the semi-dark hallway as I sat there trying to read a Ray Bradbury book I had brought along while my phone was charging. A few people slept inside just down the hall from me. It was almost impossible to read because of the poor light, which worried me because reading at night is my way to relax and fall asleep.

I checked my phone. It was 85 percent charged. *Good enough*, I thought. Before walking outside to my tent, I checked Instagram, read a few things online, watched some TikTok posts and even checked Facebook. I had gotten two more likes and Dipper commented on my post. "*I forgot about the bike ride. Good luck. Do you go Lake Placid to Albany in one day?*"

I just shook my head in that semi-dark hallway. Typical Dipper thinking we would bike almost 200 miles in one day.

My dad never responded.

CHAPTER 3

DAY 1 – LAKE PLACID
TO TUPPER LAKE (48 MILES)

Maybe I got four hours of sleep that first night. My tent was so hot, and there was some old guy in a tent near us snoring so loudly that he kept waking me up. Halfway through the night, a thunderstorm brought lots of lightning and rain and wind. My mom yelled over, asking if I was okay.

"I'm okay," I yelled back.

When her alarm went off, I pretended not to hear it. Maybe she'd let me sleep another half hour, but my mother is not the type to let anyone sleep a bit longer. I never missed the school bus a day in my life. If I was going to school, she always had me ready to go fifteen minutes early. That's just her way, and today was no different. Minutes after her cell phone alarm went off, her tent zipper went down and she was up taking down her tent. How could she always be so perky in the morning?

"Hey, sleepyhead, how are you doing in there?"

More tent zippers and more alarms and more people taking down their tents. "Why do we have to get up so early?" I tried to sit up in the tiny tent, but had to move to the center so my head wouldn't hit the ceiling.

Amid the clack of collapsing tent poles, she called out, "We want to get an early breakfast and start biking before it gets too hot."

"We do? I don't remember you asking me." I stretched out and pulled on my new blue biking shorts. I have never worn anything so tight in my life. It was like they were painted on, and then I crawled out from under my sleeping bag. I tried to pull my running shirt down over my bike shorts to cover up what seemed a bit too revealing. My neck and back were sore. I'm sure the comfy campers had no neck or back pains. I moved my head around to loosen it up in the somewhat cool air of the Adirondack morning. The sun was just coming up from behind some mountain giving off a nice orange-yellow glow. Maybe half of the tents were in the process of being taken down, but my mom moved at hyperspeed, putting her tent away. It looked like she had been up for hours. She was already wearing her black biking shorts and her light blue bike shirt, with a plastic wind breaker.

As I crawled through the narrow opening of the tent flap, my hand slipped on the slick grass. "It's wet out here," I complained.

"Yeah, didn't you hear the rain last night?" She said with a smile, putting the rest of her tent away.

The weather didn't seem as muggy, which was nice, but my feet were wet and even a bit muddy. I've never liked having wet feet. It's one of the things I dislike about running cross country. Actually, it's the only thing I dislike about running cross country.

"I'm going to use the bathroom and brush my teeth," said my mom. "Do you remember how to take down your tent?"

I waved her on and nodded that I knew what to do. Taking it down was the easy part. As she walked away, I stuck my head back inside the tent to pack up my sleeping bag and pad. I also took my cell phone from the nylon storage compartment in the corner of the tent. My dad had sent me a text message around midnight. I guess I didn't hear it because it was on vibrate.

Good luck. Sounds like fun. I'm in front of the grand jury tomorrow. Let me know how the day goes.

That's all, I thought. I also got two more likes on my Instagram post.

By the time my mom came back, I had taken down the tent flap and was trying to fit all the tent poles together. It was a lot more tricky than it looked. "Do you need some help?"

One pole was about twenty feet long and just about to touch one of the tents nearby. "Yes, can you grab the end of the pole?"

Ever so gracefully, my mom reached out for the pole, and like a professional magician, made a few quick movements with her hands and closed it up for me. "Let's pack up our tents in the big storage bag, and then pack your clothes in your bag. We'll drop everything off in the truck over there and go to breakfast."

This was a lot to process at 6:30 in the morning, and I really struggled with loading everything in the bag. My mother was invaluable—she knew just where every item should go. Was it because she was a math teacher? Was this just another geometry problem to her?

"Well, how are my two favorite bikers doing?" It was that Canadian guy Jacques. He was wearing black bike shorts and a 'I biked the Erie Canal' green and yellow bike shirt. His friend Murray shuffled along behind him. It looked like Murray wasn't too happy waking up so early either.

"We're doing great," said my mom as she stuffed my tent flap into our large storage bag. "And good morning to you."

"We have a wonderful day to begin our bike trip into your country's largest eastern wilderness," Jacques said with a big smile that appeared as forced and formal as his words.

"I guess that's true," said my mom, zipping up the bag. "The Adirondacks are very remote, especially where we'll be biking."

"Can we help with your bags? They look very heavy."

My mom smiled again, now stuffing my clothes into my bag. "No, we've got it. We'll see you at breakfast."

Jacques nodded his head. "We'll save you a spot at our table." Murray gave a sort of half-wave and followed him toward the cafeteria.

When they left, my mom went into her drill sergeant mode. "Do you have your bike shoes? Cell phone? Wallet? Rain jacket? Bike gloves? Water bottle?"

She just kept going on and on, even as we carried the three bags to the truck and packed them away with everyone else. As we walked down the truck ramp, we passed by Taylor, the girl I had met briefly the day before. "Hi, Kevin," she said with an awkward smile.

"Oh, hi," I said.

"This is my grandfather."

Her grandfather looked like an old baseball catcher. He had a grey beard and short stocky legs and very strong arms with veins sticking out. I knew not to mess with him. I nodded my head and mumbled a hello.

"Kevin is the good runner I told you about," she said to her grandfather, and then she looked back at me. "Well, I guess we'll see you out there."

On Your Left | 41

"Okay, we'll see you." I kept my head down and continued walking toward breakfast. I tried not to smile, and was practically biting my lips together.

As we walked away from the truck, my mom said. "Well, it looks like you made a friend."

I didn't want to look at my mother, but I knew she was smiling. "Yeah, I met her yesterday. She's a cross country runner."

I opened the door for her, and we entered the school. "I'm glad you both have that in common."

"I'm gonna go to the bathroom before I eat," I said, still trying not to smile.

"I love how you didn't introduce me at all. If you want to bike with her one day, that's okay with me."

I didn't say anything.

"I'll save you a seat inside."

When I got inside the bathroom, I looked in the mirror and tried not to smile, but no matter what I did, my mouth kept turning up at the ends. Why was I smiling? Did I like that girl? How could I like someone I just met? I had never felt this way about a girl before, and I've only known her for like fifteen minutes. What was wrong with me?

Breakfast wasn't bad. Pancakes and hash browns. Bike director Al went around to every table and handed out sheets of paper with the route all typed out. It had mile marks and information about big 'up hills' and 'down hills', and on the back was information about the history of Lake Placid and Saranac Lake and Paul Smith's College and Tupper Lake.

As we drank our coffee, Al got on a cheap-sounding microphone that occasionally shorted out. He told us the weather forecast and gave us some instructions about a few of the roads we'd be biking on. "All the traffic will be stopped on Main Street at 8:00 a.m.," he said, "but when you take that left on Route 86, be aware of your surroundings. We'll try to control the traffic as much as we can, but once you're out of town, get on your right and stay inside the white lines."

I was now starting to get nervous. We were really going to do this. Why did I ever post anything on Facebook and Instagram? Now I had to finish no matter what. People back home knew I was doing this. They'd ask me about it when I'd show up at the first XC practice in August.

"Earth to Kevin! Are you there?"

I came out of my trance to find my mother seated in the middle of her new Canadian friends. "What?"

"Jacques just asked if you've ever biked fifty miles before."

I took a sip of coffee. I hated drinking out of those Styrofoam cups, and this coffee was just awful. But taking a sip gave me a chance to pause before answering him. "No. I did thirty once."

Jacques didn't even seem to notice that I had said anything, as he went right back to talking with my mom. He was sitting awfully close to her. I think he must have slid a foot closer to her since I joined them. I then looked up and saw Taylor in line getting something to drink. "I'm gonna get another cup," I said and disappeared from the table.

I tried to act smooth when I saw her. "Pretty good coffee, isn't it?" What a dumb thing to say. She'd see right through me at the first sip.

"I don't know," she said. "I never drink the stuff. I'm getting a cup for my grandfather."

Whew! I breathed an invisible sigh of relief. She'd never know how bad it was.

She gave me a sort of half smile. "Well, this will be my second cup." Why was I bragging that it was my second cup to someone who doesn't drink coffee? Was I trying to act macho or something? I've never acted macho a day in my life. I moved the cup around with my right hand, and some of the coffee swirled out and burned my thumb and index finger. I tried not to grimace and slowly took the cup with my left hand and wiped the hot coffee on my bike shorts. "Have you ever biked fifty miles before?" Another smooth line. I was sounding like James Bond.

"A few times," she said. She poured the coffee into the Styrofoam cup like she had been doing this her whole life. "You probably shouldn't drink too much coffee. We have a long way to go, and it's pretty warm, even after that rain."

"Good point," I said. "I'll only take a little bit more." I had never talked about coffee this much in my life. She handed me the coffee container, and I tried to pour slowly so the coffee wouldn't spill out onto the table like it did earlier when I poured my first cup. "So you must bike a lot then, huh?"

Taylor shrugged. "I find it's a good way to cross train. In the summer, when it's so hot, I like to bike with my grandfather. We've done some fifty- and sixty-mile rides, but never anything as hilly as what we'll do this week. But, hey, we're runners, we can handle it." She then waved and began walking back to her table.

"See ya out there," I said, stupidly giving her a wave with my hand holding the hot coffee, which again swirled out of the cup and over my thumb and down my wrist. I took every muscle I had to hold my smile and not grimace in pain.

○

A few minutes later, Mom and I were back outside. It was just 8:00 a.m., and traffic had been momentarily stopped on Main Street. Since we had already loaded our bike bags with our jackets and cell phones, we were able to push our bikes in a line of other early bird bikers in the direction of Main Street.

Once we got to Main Street, I looked back at the high school and saw a few tents that had still not been taken down, those slackers. It felt sort of exciting to be on this major road in Lake Placid and have no cars moving by. I felt like I was in a road race. My mom and I were about three rows behind the first row of bikers. That first row looked to be a group of serious cyclists. Most of them were stretching in their matching shirts and shorts. Some of them were wearing those uni-suits with the shorts and shirt all connected. That old guy from Virginia, was lined up like he wanted to bolt into the lead.

Race Director Al walked to the center of the road with a bullhorn. He still sounded boring, even while shouting. "Remember, this is not a race. Follow the police escort out of town, take your time, and enjoy your ride." He went on and on again about all the places we'd be seeing. I felt like I was on a cruise ship. He encouraged us to stop and visit the towns along the way, take pictures of the beautiful scenery, and meet the native Adirondackers. At least I think that's what he said. The bullhorn made a loud screeching noise about every other word.

Three police cruisers sat in front of us ready to go, their lights flashing. I turned around and saw hundreds of cyclists behind me riding all sorts of bikes, from tandems to recumbents, from big to small, and suddenly I was very excited to get this ride on the road. My racing instincts were taking over.

Somehow, in some mom way, my mother sensed this because she tapped me on the shoulder and said, "We're gonna take this easy."

And that's when a police siren sounded and we were off!

For the last two Thanksgivings, I've been running a Turkey Trot race in Troy. It's a 3.1-mile race through that old industrial town, and moving slowly down Main Street in Lake Placid made me feel like I was back in that crowded road race, except instead of slow runners on all sides of me, I had slow bikers. For the first one hundred yards or so I was petrified. I was so worried that somebody would knock into me and I'd fall, and then one hundred cyclists behind me would fall and I'd break my arm and leg and possibly my neck. For years I had seen pictures of large groups of cyclists in races in Europe climbing up and down hills at unbelievable speeds mere inches from each other, and here I was worried about knocking into a slow biker on Main Street in Lake Placid.

But I didn't fall, and after a hundred yards or so, I could really begin pedaling. Gaps quickly opened between the cyclists, though we tried to stay close to each other. I attempted to look around at the town of Lake Placid—to see it from a new perspective—but I was so worried about hitting someone's bike tire or landing in a pot hole that I kept my eyes focused primarily on where I was going.

Every so often I would hear a few people clapping or yelling out some support from the sidewalk, but I just kept looking at what the bikers around me were doing. I didn't trust any of them.

The further we biked, the more we put some distance between us and the other bikers, until finally I was actually pedaling and not just applying my brakes every few seconds. As we turned left up a hill and away from Main Street, I finally had a clear path ahead of me, and I stood up to pedal the steep uphill. I've always loved biking up hills, and without really trying I was moving by one biker after another. It felt like the start of a cross country race as I found my groove and moved to the front of the pack. I was eating up that hill. While other cyclists struggled and strained, I could feel my legs coming to life. No, roaring to life. My heart pounded, yet I felt so alive, like this was what I had been put on this earth to do.

People at school sometimes ask why I like to run long distances. The answer is simple: it's the best feeling in the world. When I'm running on a trail in a park or a lonely country road and the only sound I hear is my feet hitting the ground, it feels like I can run forever. And if I can run forever, maybe I can live forever. But if you're not a runner, you have no idea what all that means, so usually I just say, "It's fun."

Well, charging up that hill on my way to Saranac Lake was fun. I was in such a trance that I had forgotten about my mom. It took several minutes, when

I finally crested the hill and raced a slightly downhill stretch, I eased up a bit and looked for her. Bikers slowly moved by me, until we came to a point with a police car in the center of the road. He stood outside his vehicle pointing for the bikers to move to the right. "Stay to the right!" he shouted.

Although I was warmed up and ready to go, I still tried to ease back my pace and wait for my mom to catch up. We were biking by restaurants and motels, and it was pretty much ugly America. It could have looked like just about anywhere, except every so often you'd see some beautiful mountains lurking behind the ugly storefronts. I also loved the big, puffy white clouds overhead. Cars zoomed by on my left, the drivers looking at us, trying to figure out what in the world was going on. Every so often a biker would call out from behind, "On your left," and then they'd race past me.

Just when I was beginning to wonder where my mother was, I heard her voice behind me. "I can't believe how fast you took off up that hill," she said through some heavy breathing.

There were too many cars around for us to bike next to each other, but I turned my head slightly to the left to look back at her. "I didn't mean to," I said. "I love uphills."

"That's okay. Don't feel like you have to wait for me."

I knew my mom meant that. She's never been the overprotective, clingy type, and she's never forced me to act a certain way. Even this bike ride, although it was her idea—she would have been fine if I didn't come along. "I've never biked fifty miles, ever, so I like the pace we're going now. I'm not going to race it."

We biked like that for five or six miles. We must have been biking about fifteen miles an hour, and the bikers had spread out quite a bit by now. Every so often, a biker came along and passed us, and we'd do the same to a slow biker ahead of us, but mostly we just biked along easily, looking at the scenery, watching the road and the potholes, and occasionally taking a swig of water. The farther we went from Lake Placid, the more trees we passed. After about eight miles, we came to the town of Saranac Lake.

"Pull over," said my mom. We pulled to the shoulder of the road, heading for the shade of a tall evergreen tree. She read about Saranac Lake from the paper Al gave everyone. "Let's see… 'In 1876, Dr. Livingston Trudeau built an Adirondack Cottage Sanitarium for patients suffering from tuberculosis. Several famous people, including author Robert Louis Stevenson, came to take in the mountain air.' It says here Stevenson's cottage is still standing down on Church Street. I guess there's a sign we can find to show where that is."

Some bikers zoomed by us, slowing just long enough to ask if we needed any help. It felt weird for me to just stop on the side of the road with other bikers cruising by. It's something I would never do as a runner. We waved them on, and I took another gulp of water as my mom continued reading. "That lake over there is Lake Flower." She pointed to our right. "Mark Twain vacationed there in 1901, and Albert Einstein used to vacation there every summer beginning in 1936."

My competitive fires were beginning to get to me, and I didn't like all these bikers shooting by us. "Let's get going," I said.

"It was a big bootlegging community in the 1920's, and the gangster Legs Diamond used to come up here. You know that comic strip, *Doonesbury*? Well, the creator is Garry Trudeau, and he grew up in this town."

"Hi, Kevin, are you okay?" It was Taylor and her grandfather.

I smiled knowing my mom would stop talking about this town for a few minutes. "Yeah, I'm getting a history lesson on Saranac Lake."

"I know this town pretty well," said her grandfather. "Bike with us, and I'll point out a few things."

"Please don't get him going about all the underground railroad houses in the Adirondacks," laughed Taylor.

"You mean like with slaves?" I asked, never thinking slaves would have been taken to the Adirondacks.

Taylor's grandfather laughed. "I prefer to call them enslaved people, and, yes, there are many, but I will spare you the lecture."

"Thank you," laughed Taylor.

The last thing I wanted was more on Saranac Lake, but if Taylor was going to ride, I guess I could too. I hopped on my bike, ready to go, while Mom took her time folding the paper before placing it back in her bike bag. "That would be great. I'm Jenny, and this is my son Kevin." She reached out to shake his hand.

"James McCabe, and I've heard all about what a good runner Kevin is."

I kind of rolled my eyes, my face getting red. "I'm not such a good runner."

"Oh, yes, you are," laughed Taylor as she slowly biked away.

The four of us took a slow detour through Saranac Lake, while Taylor's grandfather pointed out where the Trudeau Center was and some of the cottages and a fancy-looking place called Knollwood Manor. "I used to be a Schenectady cop," said Mr. McCabe, "and when I retired about ten years ago I finally had the time to pursue what always was my hobby and that was history."

My mom was nodding her head. "I'm a math teacher, but I also love history. Nonfiction is my favorite genre to read."

"There's so much history in the area where we live," said Mr. McCabe.

"That's one of the reasons why I wanted to take this bike trip," said my mom. "The pamphlet said we'd go through these historic Adirondack towns and learn about the area."

"Exactly," said Mr. McCabe, "and I also wanted this one to take a week and get away from using that stupid cell phone."

Taylor smiled and shook her head. "I don't use my phone any more than the rest of my friends."

"We're all addicted to them," said my mom.

"Now I can only use my phone after the ride ends," said Taylor. "That was our agreement."

"I'll follow that rule," I said even though I was not as addicted to my phone as most of the people my age were.

"Too bad we just started this ride because I'd love to spend a night here and really get a sense of this town" said my mom. She and Taylor's grandfather seemed to be hitting it off just great, and I loved biking with Taylor. After we left town, we turned back onto Route 86 going west. We were now a group of four, and there were some parts of the road with a big enough shoulder that we could ride next to each other. I loved biking next to Taylor. It felt like a date as we biked along talking about the road and the mountains and the streams. Some of my track friends had dates all the time and would talk about them, but there was never any girl that seemed to like me at school, and the girls I liked were popular with everyone else, so why would they want to go on a date with me?

"What grade are you going in?" I asked.

"I'll be a senior."

"Me, too. Are you excited about senior year?"

"I'm excited about the fall cross country season, but college scares me a bit," she said. "I like so many things. I'm not sure what I want to major in and if I should stay at a college in the area or live away."

I wanted to tell her I was also worried but not about college. I was worried my parents might break up. I changed the subject to a happier topic. "What's your favorite cross country course to run?"

My mom and Mr. McCabe were also talking away behind us, and if this was what the five-day bike ride was going to be like, then I never wanted it to end. I wanted to keep going west all the way to the Pacific Ocean. The truth was I sort of forgot about my mom and Taylor's grandfather. They were a bit behind us, but I was enjoying just cycling next to Taylor even if we weren't talking all that much. Just being beside her was great, and at times I even forgot to look around at the lush green scenery. We must have been going pretty fast because we seemed to be passing a lot of bikers.

We had a tough two-mile climb around mile 12, and no one talked for about ten minutes, but then the road leveled out again and we got back into formation, talking and laughing, and soon we were on Route 30 going north through the stone gates of Paul Smith's College.

"Hotel management was a big major at Paul Smith's," shouted Mr. McCabe from behind us. "I can't wait to see what kind of food they offer us."

It was a few minutes past 10:00 when we biked onto the grounds of the college, and even though it was such a beautiful campus, with the Lower St. Regis gleaming a bright blue right in its center, what we were really looking for was some food.

"Look at those buildings," said Taylor. "It's almost like they're mansions or something."

There was a big tent in the center of this enormous green lawn right in front of the St. Regis. About fifty bikers stood under the tent eating, drinking, and laughing.

"This campus is gorgeous," said my mom.

We rested our bikes against a few trees and walked toward the giant white tent. It was nice to take off our bike helmets and bike gloves. My shirt was pretty sweaty, but all I cared about was getting something good to eat.

"It's weird," said Taylor, placing her bike helmet on top of her bike. "When I go for a long run, I never get hungry. I just want to drink water, or maybe Gatorade, but when I go for a long bike ride, I always get hungry."

Fortunately, our hunger would be satisfied inside that tent. They had six different kinds of cookies, plus brownies, a wide variety of fruit, energy bars, and even some candy, like Twizzlers and Snickers. "Try some of our pizza," said a student with long brown hair held back by a headband that made him look like he had just come from Woodstock in 1969.

The four of us grabbed as much food as we could carry and filled our water bottles with some Gatorade, then found a few empty Adirondack chairs out near the dock by the water.

"This is a nice break," said Mr. McCabe.

We chewed our food and nodded our heads in agreement. It was nice to sit down and look at the water on this amazing campus built like an Adirondack camp surrounded by water and mountains. I took a picture with my cell phone of the water and the mountains behind and quickly posted a comment on Facebook. *I made it to our first rest stop at Paul Smith's College. 21 miles down and 27 more to Tupper Lake.*

We didn't say much sitting there. Sometimes it's just great to sit quietly and look at what's in front of you. That's probably why I like to run by myself most of the time. When I run with someone else, I feel like I have to talk to them, but when I'm all alone, I notice things more and pay attention better to what's going on around me. Today, just sitting there, I noticed the sun reflecting off the water, the birds singing, the sound of the water hitting the dock, and the big puffy white marshmallow clouds in the sky. And I noticed that Taylor looked like an excellent runner.

"Well, you got here in a hurry. I figured you were a fast biker, but I didn't think you'd be that fast." It was Jacques, with Murray standing behind him as usual like a secret service agent. They dripped sweat and drank what was left in their water bottles.

My mom turned around and waved. "Welcome. You've got to try some of their pizza."

Taylor and her grandfather just smiled at them.

It's not that I minded Jacques and Murray, it was just that I had been enjoying our time, just the four of us, without interruption. Jacques and Murray reminded me of noise, and how much they liked my mom reminded me of my dad, and that made me sad. Jacques said a few more things to my mom, but I wasn't paying much attention to them. If I did, it would have made me sadder still, or perhaps angry. I don't know why angry, but I found myself wrapping my knuckles around the wide arm of the Adirondack chair the more Jacques spoke. When they finally walked away to get some food, I said to my mom, "I forgot to tell you that dad sent me a text late last night wishing us good luck. He wants to hear all about how we do today."

My mom smiled and took a long sip from her water bottle. "I got the same text."

"It's going to be tough to leave this spot," said Mr. McCabe "We have twenty-seven more miles, and a lot of up and down on Route 30, till we get to Tupper Lake."

My mom shielded her eyes against the sun as she looked back toward our bikes. "And the way that sun is peaking out of those clouds, it's going to be hot. I doubt we'll have much shade on Route 30."

Taylor stood up, apparently eager to go. I imagined how wonderful it would be to reach out and take her hand and ease her back down to the chair so we could sit here a little while longer. I imagined how soft and warm that hand must feel. My dad never took my mom's hand in his anymore. I remember as a kid, on some of our Cape Cod beach vacations, the three of us would walk the beach, and my parents would hold hands. Even though I was just a little kid, I liked when they did that.

Instead of leaving right away, we walked around the campus for a while, and I wondered what college I'd end up attending. The buildings resembled those old Adirondack camps with gigantic wooden beams and big windows rich people used to build, but the architecture wasn't the only thing I liked. It was nice to use a clean bathroom and not one of those disgusting port-a-potties. It was also nice to take your time and not have someone pounding on the stall door asking, "Is anyone in there?"

It was almost 11:00 a.m., and bikers were still coming in for rest and refreshments when the four of us decided to get back on our bikes and continue our trek.

We followed the yellow marks on the road, which took us back to Route 30, known to the locals as Blue Mountain Road. The road went mostly up and down, with a decent shoulder for us to ride. Quite a few big sixteen-wheeler trucks blew past us almost knocking me off my bike a few times, and because there were so many cars, the four of us decided to bike single-file.

At about twelve miles from Paul Smith's, there was a water break on the side of the road. We stopped just long enough to get some water, eat a few granola bars, and go to the bathroom. After thirty-three miles of biking in the heat, and with fifteen more miles to go, we weren't in a very talkative mood—except Taylor. She liked to talk. Perhaps she was as nervous as me?

"Have you ever been to the Wild Center?" asked Taylor. She must have been as tired and as hot as me, but she still looked as nice and as fresh as she did earlier that morning when she poured a coffee for her grandfather.

"Is that where we're having dinner?" I asked. The calf of my right leg was cramping, so I was trying to stretch it. Despite the pain, I was excited to be talking to this pretty girl. I biked more miles today than ever before, and I hadn't felt like this since I completed my first five-mile distance run with the team a few years ago. I wanted to celebrate—let out a whoop, maybe give Taylor a fist bump. Instead I just played it cool and kept our conversation going. Although I'm not very good at small talk, I was trying.

"It's this really nice museum that explains how the Adirondacks were formed," said Taylor "They also have some nice hiking trails there."

"I've been meaning to go there," said my mom. "I hear it's done very well."

"Well, maybe we could tour it together before dinner. Or after. It's free for the bikers tonight, isn't it?" Taylor said. She must have read all the information that guy Al gave out earlier today.

"Taylor, Kevin and his mom may have other plans," said Mr. McCabe.

"Oh, no, we'd love to tour the place with you," I said sounding a bit too eager.

Mom looked at me with a raised eyebrow.

Back on the bikes, we continued through the beautiful mountain scenery. The biggest hill we had to conquer happened right at the end as we headed into the town of Tupper Lake. I broke away from the group as I charged up the hill. I didn't do it to make a point, it's just the only way I know how to bike up hills—by standing up on the bike and pedaling with all my strength in both my legs and my arms. And the great thing was that Taylor decided to go right with me. It's not like we were racing, not exactly, but we were putting in some effort, two distance runners who liked to work hard and get their hearts pumping. At the top of the hill we stopped and looked back at my mom and Mr. McCabe who were straining up the hill about one hundred yards away. "That was fun," said Taylor and she gave me a fist bump. It was the best fist bump I had ever gotten.

Tupper Lake looked sort of rundown, but the lake to our right sure was pretty, with boats sailing on it and mountains rising from behind. It didn't take long to come upon Tupper Lake High School, and after searching for about fifteen minutes to find the right location to pitch our tents, we dropped our bikes and walked to the truck holding our bags.

"What makes a good tent location?" I asked.

"A dry area," said my mom.

"I like to find a place where you can get a nice breeze," said Mr. McCabe. "I also want to be away from the other tents."

"But you don't want to be too far from the school just in case you need to visit the bathroom at night," said my mother, and we all laughed.

We were some of the first bikers to arrive at the school, and even though I was exhausted, I didn't complain about carrying the tent and luggage, or putting up the tent. It took about thirty minutes, but finally we were ready to shower up and put on some dry clothes.

"Apparently they have showers inside the school," said my mom, "but I'd encourage you to use the shower truck. I found the water to be nice and warm yesterday."

There didn't seem to be anyone waiting in line at the truck, and since I was sweaty, and my calf was a bit sore, I knew the warm water would feel awfully good.

"Mrs. Walsh, I'll walk over with you." It was Taylor. She was crawling out of the tent she shared with her grandfather about ten feet away from my tent. She was carrying a running bag she must have gotten at some road race in Vermont.

My mom smiled. "That would be great."

I always felt kind of sorry for my mom because there was no girl in our house. Sometimes she'd buy a new dress or a new sweater and model it for me and Dad. "It's great," we'd say with false enthusiasm, but what we really wanted to do was go back to watching TV or listening to music, or whatever we had been doing. Taylor complemented a shirt my mom was carrying to change into, and it sure was more genuine than anything my dad and I had ever said.

"Kevin, remember to get your clean towel at that desk. Just tell them your name, and they'll look it up. After when you're done with your shower, bring the towel back."

I gave her a thumbs up and took one long slug from my water bottle. Taylor and my mom were chatting away as they walked toward the truck. I tried not to be too obvious. She had the smooth athletic way about her that was oozing with confidence. "Are you gonna shower?" It was her grandfather. I think he noticed me watching his granddaughter, and I suddenly felt a bit like some creepy, slimy sleaze ball guy.

"Yeah." I quickly went through my clothes bag to find something clean, and then I wanted to get over to that truck before Taylor's grandfather offered to join me. He seemed like a nice guy and all, but I didn't feel like walking around naked with him.

It was an easy process to get the clean towel, and soon I was walking up the steps in the shower truck. There seemed to be a lot of talking going on in there despite the roar of the showers on full blast.

I must admit that the warm water did feel spectacular, and even though I didn't like showering in a truck with five or six old guys, I knew I was going to do this every day for the next week, and if the shower was going to be this good, then it might just be all right.

The next few hours were some of the best of my life. The four of us, along with Jacques and Murray, took a short bus ride from the high school to the Wild Center. We spent an hour walking around the museum. I learned a lot about the Adirondacks and how they were formed and what animals live there. I'm not usually so 'gung ho' about these educational museums, but this place was fun, and we all loved it. It was great that only people from the bike ride were allowed in at that time so it wasn't too crowded. They showed a film of pictures by this Adirondack photographer named Carl Heilman. They were these amazing color photos of mountains and streams and lakes and all sorts of wildlife like deer and bears and eagles. At the end of the film my mom was tearing up, and Jacques seemed concerned about her. He even got her some tissues.

"It's nothing," said my mom. "The music and those photos were so beautiful. I've been to many of those places, and the photos brought back some good memories."

I figured she must have been thinking about my dad, and even though Jacques and Murray were being very friendly, they weren't much like my dad. I also knew some of those places like Avalanche Lake where I hiked with my parents and Mt. Marcy, another hike we completed. Those pictures brought up some good memories for me, too, but also a reminder that we haven't had fun like that in a long time.

"Does anyone want to walk on the trails?" Taylor smiled and stood with her hands on her hips.

"I will," I said very quickly, but all the adults said "No, thanks," and complained about how their feet hurt and that it was too hot. They decided to sit at some tables outside the museum by a pond. There was another wine and cheese party going on there before dinner. Adults sure seemed to enjoy hanging out and eating cheese and drinking wine. The trail seemed like more fun.

"We won't be gone too long," said Taylor, though I wasn't sure if she was addressing my mother or her grandfather.

My mom smiled, still clutching her tissue. "Have

a good time," she said, looking me right in the eyes and giving a slight nod.

When Taylor and I were out of earshot, we started talking. "I came here last summer with my grandfather. The trail is short, but would be great to run on, don't you think?"

"That's my favorite kind of running. On trails, I mean."

"During cross country, our coach drives us in a van out to the Pine Bush, and they have all these sandy trails that we run up and down on. I love running there. I could run all day on trails like that."

I loved walking with Taylor. We talked about running, and other places we've visited where the running was good. We also talked about how much running and biking were alike. I wanted time to just stop so we could stay like this forever, walking down this green trail with the sun flashing on and off between the leaves. I only met her yesterday, but I was already thinking how much I wanted to have running dates with her when we got back home, maybe at the Pine Bush up and down those sandy trails, and then go have ice cream someplace. I couldn't wait to see her at those big Saturday cross-country meets in the fall. Now that I knew who she was, I'd cheer her on during her race, and she'd cheer for me when I ran. That's what some of the runners on my team did—the ones who were dating, I mean. It was like they had their own private cheering fan club. Dwight had a group of people cheering for him like he was a Hollywood celebrity or something. Even the guys I was much faster than would have their girlfriends out on the course with signs. They'd clap for me, but when their boyfriend ran by behind me they'd scream and shout and encourage him like he had a chance to win the entire race.

"This sure is pretty back here." We were walking beneath gigantic evergreen trees, and the ground was soft with only a few tree roots.

"A little further on it comes to the Raquette River, and they have a wooden dock."

I wanted to reach out and take her hand. In the movies, with the violin music playing, those smooth guys always seemed to know the right time to take that girl's hand in theirs. It's the same way when I'm running a race. There have been many times when I was too afraid to pick up the pace and make a move near the finish line. In a lot of my races, I've been content to just cruise in for second or third place behind one of my teammates. My coach knows what I'm doing and has often said, "Kevin, if you're feeling good, go for it. Don't settle. Don't just finish a race when you can go faster." I guess I'm afraid of failing. Second or third place is pretty good, and I fear that maybe if I pushed too hard for the win, I might lose all my energy and finish way back, or even drop out.

We could see the water now and the dock, my heart was pounding so hard that I thought it would beat its way out of my chest. Taylor was talking and I was trying to listen, but I couldn't focus. I kept wondering when was the right time to take her hand? Was it too soon? We had only just met. Was there ever a right time to do something like that, to take a girls hand in yours? I decided to make my move. I reached out my right hand to take her hand in mine, and that's when her cell phone rang.

"I have to take this," Taylor said. "It's my boyfriend."

CHAPTER 4

DAY 2 - TUPPER LAKE TO
BLUE MOUNTAIN LAKE (32 MILES)

I was stunned. I must have looked like a zombie as we walked back into the wine and cheese party. Taylor had a boyfriend! Of course she did. Anyone who looked like her, had that smile and was so smart would! Why would I ever think she'd be interested in me? I'm tall and awkward, like some laboratory experiment gone horribly wrong. An escapee from a freak show. My hair is untamable. I have pimples all over my face, and my chest is so scrawny you could eat a bowl of cereal out of it. Why would someone like Taylor ever think about dating something like me? And just like when I'm at home with my parents, and they're sitting around driving each other crazy, I suddenly wanted to put on my Nike running shoes and run till I collapsed. To run as far away as I could, and when I got there, I wanted to just keep going.

My mom knew something was wrong as soon as Taylor and I joined her and her three male friends at a long table under a large tent. They had a Brooks Barbecue of chicken and potatoes and salad and rolls. I chewed the food, but I don't remember if it had any taste. I forced a few smiles and tried to laugh at some of Jacques' corny jokes, but what I really wanted to do was crawl into my sleeping bag and disappear into my tent.

"Are you feeling okay?" my mom whispered to me.

"Tired," I said and shrugged my shoulders.

I've never been good at hiding my feelings. From anyone. Even Taylor gave me a concerned look. She tried to get me back into the conversation by joking around, but I wasn't biting. I think I gave her the same half smile I gave Jacques's jokes, which were getting worse by the minute.

After dinner, they brought in some guy in his twenties with long, scraggy dark hair and a thick beard who played indie folk music on an acoustic guitar. We all sat around on benches and chairs and listened to him. He mostly sang songs about people falling out of love or having the one you love die in some horrible way. This was just what I wanted to hear. Jacques was all geared up, telling us about our next day's ride to Blue Mountain Lake, but I wasn't really paying attention.

I spent most of the night thinking how stupid I was to ever believe someone like Taylor Lewis might be interested in me. My Aunt Agnes always says my body is trying to catch up to the size of my big feet. My hair is sort of curly, and I haven't been able to control it since I let it grow out when I was a freshman, and I sometimes wonder what sort of picture I could make if I connected all the pimples on my face. Also, I'm not the type of guy who can get a girl to laugh. What I can do is run, even if that means running away from them.

While the guitar dude kept playing depressing music, I told my mom I was going inside to the bathroom. What I really wanted to do was call my dad. It was 7:20 on a Sunday night, so hopefully he'd be home. He picked up on the third ring.

"Well, I was expecting to hear from you guys," he said. "How was day one?"

I told him the ride was forty-eight miles and that we just finished dinner and were now listening to music at the Wild Center.

"You sound tired," he said. "How do your legs feel?" I could tell he was scrolling through something on his laptop while he was talking to me.

"I'm kind of tired. My legs feel good, though." I wanted to tell him that my heart was broken. "Do you miss us?"

He was quiet for a few seconds. "I miss you and Mom very much." Neither of us spoke for a while and then he said, "I think I made a big mistake not coming with you."

"Our last day, we bike from the Saratoga Battlefield to Albany. It's only something like twenty-five miles. Maybe you can bike with us that day."

He gave a sort of slow yawn. "Well, let's see—that's Thursday. I'd really love to bike with you, but I'm scheduled to present to the grand jury again." He gave an odd, almost condescending sort of corny chuckle. "It's kind of a big thing."

"Yeah, sure, I get it." I wanted to scream at him that if he kept putting his job ahead of everything, then soon the only thing he'd have would be that stupid job. "Well, I better get back."

"Good luck tomorrow. You're staying at the Adirondack Museum, aren't you? Remember how much fun we had there?"

My eyes were getting watery. For someone who didn't come on our trip, he seemed to know exactly what we were doing every day. "I'll call you tomorrow."

"Tell your mom I love her."

"You should tell her that," I said, and then pressed end. I even just shut my entire phone off in case he tried to call back. It might have been the meanest thing I've ever said to anyone, but I sort of felt good about it.

When I came back outside, I informed everyone that I needed to charge up my phone. I could tell that Taylor was about to offer to join me, but I left in a hurry before she or anyone could say anything.

I looked all around the Wild Center for any type of electrical outlet to charge my phone. I found one at the far end of the museum in a darkened section near a tank filled with a dozen or more fish native to the Adirondacks. A security guard walked over and saw what I was doing. I figured I was going to get the big lecture about not being inside the museum alone. "How'd the ride go today?" he asked.

"My butt's sore," I said. "Can I charge up here?"

"No problem," he said, smiling and walking on. What a cool security guard, I thought. He reminded me of Rusty, a hall monitor we have at the high school. Rusty is like eighty or something, but he knows every kid in that building, always has time to talk and the kids respect him, even the toughest kids in the school. When Rusty tells you to get back to class or to be quiet in the hall, you do it. It's like he cares about you. For a while today I was thinking that Taylor really cared about me, but that was before I knew she had a boyfriend.

I just stood there and stared at these trout and perch as they stared back at me. They looked lonely in there, and when they swam by and looked at me, I wondered how I looked to them. They looked at me the way most people in my school look at me, like I'm not there, like they see right through me, like I'm not important.

Twenty minutes later, I turned my phone back on. My dad had called back two times, but I was too tired to call him now. I didn't even play back his voicemail messages. As my phone charged, I read some email and looked through some Facebook and Instagram entries. It seemed like everyone back home was having fun going to the movies and running together. Did they even remember I was on a bike trip in the Adirondacks? As I skimmed through some posts, Dipper sent me a message in real time.

How goes it Mr Adirondack biker?

I wrote back to him: *A little sore. 48 miles today!*

Wow! When do you finish and where?

Although I sat alone in a dark museum in the middle of the Adirondacks, I didn't feel so lonely now. *Thursday. Albany at the Corning Preserve.*

IDK where that is.

Tomorrow we're biking 32 miles to Blue Mountain Lake.

IDK where that is either.

As usual, Dipper had me laughing. *You gotta get out more.*

Gotta go. Have to pick pizza at Luiggi's. Hopefully Gabby will be there Good luck tomorrow.

C ya. Tell Gabby you love her!

Gabby was this girl on our team that Dipper had a wicked crush on, but like every other girl on our team she seemed to only notice Dwight.

I charged my phone for about fifteen more minutes, which meant that by the time I went back outside, the hippie dude was hopefully playing his last depressing song. Leaving the museum I noticed the bright orange moon was beginning to rise in the low sky, and the adults were all sitting around and talking a bit about the next day's ride. Taylor was sitting with them, but she was reading something on her phone, probably a text from her boyfriend. I couldn't wait to get away and go to my tent. It had been a long day, and when we all got on the bus to go back to the high school, we were mostly quiet. I took a seat away from everyone in the back and just looked out the window as the bus brought us back to the high school.

I was the last one off the bus when we got back and Taylor was waiting for me. "Today was fun," she said.

I yawned. "Yeah. I'm tired." I didn't say anything the rest of the way back to our tents. I wasn't very happy, and I didn't feel like pretending that I was. I only had a few more days on this stupid bike ride and then I could get back to my running and cross country would start and I'd graduate from high school and move away to college and live happily ever after. Maybe.

As I set up my sleeping bag in my tent, my mom poked her head in to ask if everything was okay.

"Taylor has a boyfriend." I tried to whisper it so Taylor wouldn't hear. She was in the tent with her grandfather maybe ten feet away, and I could hear the two of them talking in a slightly muffled way.

"Oh, I thought it might be something like that."

We just sat there and I shrugged my shoulders.

"Anyway, today was fun, and I started thinking that maybe she could be my girlfriend. I know it's stupid. I mean I only met her yesterday, and I never had a girlfriend, and I'm seventeen…."

"It's not stupid."

"She told me her boyfriend is a soccer player. Not even a runner."

Mom smiled. "Can you imagine!"

"So I guess I was moping around a little bit."

My mom nodded her head. "Just a little."

"I called Dad."

My mom's eyebrows went up. Maybe she was part Vulcan after all "And how's he doing?"

"You know, if I was ever married to someone like Taylor, I sure wouldn't care so much about my job. I'd want to be home as much as possible." It just sort of came out, but it was too late to take back now.

Mom gave me that school guidance-counselor look like they know all the answers. "It's not always as easy as that."

We sat there in this awkward silence, and I wondered who would crack first. I also didn't feel like talking about a girl with my mom. "Well, I am kind of tired. I think I'll go inside, hit the bathroom, and come back to the tent and read for a while." Reading has always been one of my favorite ways of tuning out, particularly when things needed to be tuned out.

My mom just kept staring at me with this sort of odd smile like she was trying to figure out what to say.

"This whole girlfriend boyfriend thing is never easy. Even when you're old like me."

"I wouldn't know."

My mom slowly backed her way out of my tent. "You'll have a girlfriend someday, and it will probably be sooner than you think."

I actually slept much better that night, but once again my mom was up and taking down her tent like we were about to be invaded by an army of arm-chewing zombies. Unlike yesterday, I was up early, hoping to stay ahead of Taylor. No luck. She and her grandfather were right there, taking down their tent. "Good morning, Kevin," she said. She was wearing red and white pajama pants and a long grey cotton shirt. I've never seen anyone look so good in a long grey cotton shirt.

"Morning," I mumbled. It's kind of crazy like I liked Taylor so much that I never wanted to ever see her again, and when I saw her all I could think of was her boyfriend the soccer player. I sometimes worry I'm the most immature 17-year-old in America, and how am I even going to survive college which is quickly approaching.

Our two Canadian friends saved an entire table for us to eat breakfast with them. Jacques was practically jumping up and down to flag us over when we walked in the breakfast area. As we were eating Jacques read through the Day Two itinerary. "Basically, it's Route 30 for ten miles until it merges with Route 28N, and then on to Long Lake, about twenty-two miles away, where the first stop will be. Then it's another ten miles or so to the Adirondack Museum. We've got a big climb around Mile 13, and then a big downhill around Mile 19."

"I've gone canoeing on Long Lake before," said Taylor and she smiled at me.

I was trying to chew my oatmeal. It tasted like warmed-up paste.

"That's right. We camped out on that island for a weekend two summers ago," said Taylor's grandfather.

"Says here at twenty-two miles we're stopping at the Adirondack Hotel in the town of Long Lake," said Jacques.

"We had lunch there," said Taylor. She was getting all excited and practically about to jump out of her seat. "Do you remember how it rained on our paddle back and we couldn't wait to get off the lake and get in some dry clothes and eat lunch?"

Taylor's grandfather was smiling and holding his coffee. "We were singing songs as the rain poured down and cheering when we finally saw the hotel in the distance."

"That was about the best pizza I've ever eaten," said Taylor.

"Says here the hotel was built in 1895 and John Wayne and Mick Jagger stayed there," said Jacques.

"Did they stay there together in the same room?" laughed Murray and everyone but me laughed.

"What an odd couple that would be," laughed my mom.

And as they were all going on and on, I spied The Virginia guy pouring himself a coffee.

"Kevin, have you ever been to Tupper Lake?" Taylor asked and then took a sip from her glass of orange juice.

The Virginia guy was wearing a Boston Marathon shirt. "I'm gonna get more coffee," I said, and sprang up out of my seat to the coffee table.

The Virginia guy smiled at me when I arrived at the table. "How goes it, my young friend?"

"It's going ok," I said, taking the coffee container from his hand and pouring it into my cup. "You ran the Boston Marathon?"

"Twenty-one times now," he said with a far-off look.

"Wow. I'd love to run it someday."

He patted me on the right shoulder. "You will."

"Did you run the year of the bomb?"

He was quiet for a few seconds, then looked away. "I finished ten minutes before that bomb went off. I was complaining to a fellow runner about how slow I ran. I was actually complaining about a slow running time. After that bomb went off and I saw all the injured people and the blood, well, it reminded me how lucky I really am, and that I had absolutely nothing to complain about."

"Can I bike with you today?" I don't know why I said that. It just sort of erupted out of my mouth.

"Why, sure, young man. I'm going to try and average twenty miles an hour for the whole ride. Can you stay at that pace?"

"Sure. Yeah. I don't know. I'll try." I've never gone all-out in my bike riding, but for some reason, I wanted to try it today.

"I'll meet you out front in…" he checked his watch, "…let's say fifteen minutes. Around 7:45. Is that good?"

"I'll be there," I said, and turned and walked back to my table.

Everyone was still going on about John Wayne and Mick Jagger spending the night together in a room at the Adirondack Hotel. "Can you picture John Wayne wearing those rock 'n' roll spandex pants?" laughed Jacques. He was practically choking on orange juice. He had tears in his eyes from all the laughing.

"And wouldn't you love to see Mick Jagger wearing John Wayne's six shooter?" laughed Murray.

I leaned over to my mom and said, "I'm gonna bike with that guy from Virginia today." I nodded my head in his direction, he was now sitting with his wife on the opposite side of the caféteria.

Everyone sort of quieted down, although many of them were still out of breath from laughing. "Why do you want to bike with that guy?" asked Jacques.

"He ran the Boston Marathon. That, and he's going to go fast today, and I'm going to try and stay with him."

Mom was smiling. "Well, of course. I hope you can stay with him. We'll be going in about twenty or thirty minutes."

"I'm going at 7:45, so I better finish up fast." I didn't look at Taylor. I just sat down and tried to eat the rest of my bagel as fast as I could. Jacques and Murray went right back to cracking jokes and laughing and when I was done, I said goodbye to the group as a whole so I didn't have to talk to anyone specifically, and walked over to throw away my trash and bus my tray. My mom followed me to the trashcan.

"Are you okay?" she asked.

I nodded my head that I was just fine.

"Did Taylor say anything mean to you?"

I dumped the trash from my tray into the can and looked around to make sure no one had heard what she said. "No, she didn't say anything mean."

"Or do anything mean?"

"No."

"Then, you don't have to ignore the poor girl." She dumped her trash as if making a statement.

It felt very uncomfortable to have a secretive conversation like this in the middle of the cafeteria. "I'm not ignoring her."

We were now placing our dirty glasses and plates on a conveyor belt that brought them to the kitchen. "That girl has been asking you questions and talking to you, and you just keep giving her one-word responses. Is that how you treat a friend?"

"I guess I'm not a morning person."

My mom was now looking me directly in the face and frowning. "Do you know your father has said that same thing to me just about every morning I've been married to him?"

I looked at my watch. "I better go. I promised that old guy I'd bike with him at 7:45."

"And your father always has some place he has to rush off to. Kevin, you can't keep running away from problems. Why do you think our family is…" but then she stopped speaking. "Anyway," she took a deep breath, "have a good ride today, and I'm sorry Taylor has a boyfriend, but she's a nice girl and you should treat her kindly "

"I will," I said, and then watched my mom walk away to rejoin everyone at the table.

Sure enough, right at 7:45, there was the Virginia guy with his bike and bike helmet waiting for me. He reached his hand out to shake. "If we're going to bike together, we need to know each other's name. I'm Vern Jacobs."

I shook his warm hand. "Kevin Walsh."

We got on our bikes and slowly pedaled away. "So, Kevin Walsh, tell me what kind of a runner you are. I would have placed you as a basketball player."

That old label again. "I used to be a basketball

player." The road leading from the school took us briefly back through part of downtown Tupper Lake. It looked a bit poor and rundown. Some of the businesses were boarded up and empty. A few of the homes had Make America Great flags flying proudly. Some people on the sidewalk watched us bike by, but there was none of the excited cheering and clapping we had in Lake Placid. It looked sort of like a town in one of those post-apocalyptic movies, and any minute I expected to see a radioactive creature come charging after us snapping its teeth. "Last year as a junior, I broke 4:30 in the 1600 and 9:45 in the 3200, and I can run the 5K in a little over sixteen minutes."

As we got farther away from downtown, he began to pick up the pace. "Those are some fast times, my young friend. Let's see how you do on a bike."

He must have noticed me looking at the sad-looking town because he said, "It's a problem all over America."

"What?" I was getting a little out of breath as we picked up speed.

"This country is just getting too urbanized."

"Yeah." I was already into one-word conversations to save my energy.

"It's like this in Virginia, too. Everyone's moving to the cities, especially the young people, and what do these nice little country towns have to offer when everyone's moving away? Not much."

I liked hearing his strong Southern accent.

"A little town like this back in the '50s and '60s was a great place to grow up, and I bet there were generations of families who did that. But now the factories are closed and maybe for a few months in the summer the place comes alive with those rich people and their summer camps, but this cute town deserves more than that."

"How fast are we going?" I tried not to sound too winded.

"Eighteen. Let's pick it up to twenty. It's mostly flat for the first ten miles. Are you ready?"

I moved my neck around to loosen up a bit. "Let's go," I said.

And that's when we took off. I got in right behind him as he talked about getting into a cadence. "Cycling, like running, is all about finding a nice rhythm and keeping it there. If you run the mile in 4:30, you know what I'm talking about."

I nodded my head because I couldn't speak. If I could have, I would have told him about how much I love getting into that running rhythm where my legs just carry me, where I feel numb to the world with no worries about anything or anyone. Yeah, running usually put me in a trance, and my legs would take me where they wanted to go while my fears and worries just evaporated.

"This is a good road. A nice shoulder. Let's pick it up some more. Let's pick up that cadence."

I got right in behind him and let him do all the work. It's the same thing I noticed years ago as a runner, particularly running on the track. Even though I'm tall, I could still tuck in behind a fast runner and just keep following them, my eyes on the top of their head or the back of their neck, letting them set the fast pace. I'd concentrate so much that the laps would just fly by. The same thing was happening now on the ride to Long Lake.

There wasn't much to look at on the route—just green trees on both sides of the road and the black pavement with two yellow lines going up the middle and a bright white line separating the road from the shoulder. We were biking on the white line as much as we could and only moved to the shoulder when we heard a car or truck moving up on us. Not one bike rider went by us, and we must have passed twenty or thirty on the ride. The road condition was mostly good with only a few potholes and frost heaves, allowing me to keep my eyes on the back of Mr. Jacobs. We poured it on one mile after another, and it reminded me a bit of our long runs with the distance guys on the roads by the high school.

Distance runs featured a lot of talk and laughter, mostly about girls and who had just done the smelliest fart. Mr. Jacobs was mostly quiet. Every now and then he'd look back to see how I was doing. "We're at twenty miles per hour now," he'd scream back at me. "Can you go any faster?"

"Yes," I'd yell out, not sure if I could, but willing to give it a shot. And away we'd go.

I had driven on this road before, but I had never noticed how it would constantly go up and down the whole way. I began to wonder how my mom and Taylor were doing. Were they biking together, and were they with Jacques and Murray? Was Jacques still cracking jokes about John Wayne and Mick Jagger? It suddenly occurred to me how much fun biking was yesterday from Saranac Lake to Paul Smith's College. Today seemed more like a killer track workout of repeat 400's, but I didn't let Mr. Jacobs get away from me. Whenever he'd pull away a bit, I'd push myself to go faster and stay with him. It kind of helped me not to think about Taylor and her soccer boyfriend.

Soon I began to see a body of water on my right, which I figured must be Long Lake, or maybe some stream that emptied into the lake. More cars went by us, and the homes started showing up more regularly.

"Only another mile and we'll be at the rest stop," yelled Mr. Jacobs. He had a large sweat stain on his back, which made me feel good that he was working as hard as I was. "We're averaging 19," he screamed short of breath. "Let's get up and over twenty."

"Okay," I screamed back, putting my head down as I tried to will my legs to go faster. I had those clip-in bike shoes which helped me press the pedal down and then pull up. I had a good rhythm going.

When we finally arrived at the large, blue and grey Adirondack Hotel, I almost fell trying to get off the bike. My legs were sore, like John Wayne getting off a horse or maybe Mick Jagger after a three-hour concert. It felt like someone had been punching them for hours, and I was dizzy and thirsty.

"My young friend, you are a fine cyclist." Mr. Jacobsl was patting me on the shoulder. "We averaged 19.7. Let's have a quick stop and see if we can maintain that for ten more." I wasn't sure if I could maintain that pace for one-mile down a hill. This old codger was quite an athlete, and I needed more than a quick stop to get back out with him.

The rest area was set up across the street from the hotel on a sandy beach. There was a blue seaplane and a red and white seaplane just up the beach on the water, and the pilots stood there holding signs trying to get some of the cyclists to take a ride. Since we had ridden so fast to get here, there were only a handful of bikers on the beach filling up their bottles with Gatorade or snacking on bananas, peanut butter and granola bars. With mountains surrounding Long Lake and the blue water dotted with numerous green islands, I had to admit it was one of the most beautiful places I had ever seen. A few people sat in Adirondack rocking chairs on the hotel's long wrap-around porch watching the scattering of bikers coming down the road toward the beach. It was right around 9:00 a.m. on a Monday morning in July in the middle of the

Adirondacks when it suddenly hit me: I was very lucky indeed to be here.

"This place is great," I said a little out of breath and leaning my bike up against a tree by the beach.

Even Mr. Jacobs seemed a bit speechless. "Down in Virginia, when we think of the Adirondacks, this is what we imagine it must look like."

The two of us just stood there in the damp sand looking out into the lake that still had a mist of fog rising from its waters. I could barely make out a few islands far out into the mist-covered lake. It was mostly quiet as we drank from our water bottles, and that's when a strange high-pitched cry broke through the quiet air. I looked at Mr. Jacobs with a puzzled expression.

"I do believe that's the cry of a loon," he said.

"Really? A loon. I've never seen one of them before."

Mr. Jacobs smiled. "Well, now you can say you've heard one."

We walked over to fill up our water bottles. The cyclists in line with us were all very fit, mostly tall and strong. There was only one woman, and she was jacked like she had just completed basic training for the Marines. I was the youngest person in line, and I seemed to be sweating the most. They were all talking about what an easy ride it had been. "Mostly flat, a few turns, good shoulders—you could do this blindfolded," said a tall bald guy wearing a "I Biked Whiteface Mountain" shirt.

I took some cut-up orange chunks, filled my two water bottles with green and red Gatorade, and walked over to a bench to sit down. Mr. Jacobs followed me over and gave me a couple of chocolate chip cookies. "So you've done a few of these bike trips before," I said.

He nodded his head while chewing some cookie. "I retired five years ago, and my wife and I like to travel. We did a bike trip in Virginia from one Civil War battlefield to another, and we liked it, so we tried a few more. We usually do one every July or August when it's too hot to run."

I leaned back on the wooden bench. My shirt stuck to me even as the breeze from the lake cooled me off nicely. "How does this compare with the others?"

"Right here, with this view, well… it's just about the best I've ever seen." He was still standing by the bench and I could tell he was getting a bit edgy to get back on the bike.

"You know I've been in the backseat of a car, and I've driven by here a few times, but I never realized how pretty it is. How pretty the Adirondacks are."

Mr. Jacobs nodded his head with the wisdom of a Tibetan monk. "You can't see much in a car, but get out on your bike, or go for a hike, or put your running shoes on and go for a run, and that's when you really see what's out there and how beautiful this world is."

A steady flow of bikers was now coming in our direction in groups of two, four, and six.

He stood up. "Well, young fella, are you ready for that last ten miles?"

"You know, I think I'm gonna wait for my mom and that group and bike in with them." I don't know why I said that, but it just sort of felt like the right thing to do.

He gave me a smile. "Now that's a great idea. I truly enjoyed biking with you, my young man, and I hope we can do it again sometime this week." He then took a sip from his water bottle, pulled his right leg over his bike frame, and pedaled away down Route 30 toward Blue Mountain Lake and the Adirondack Museum.

I didn't have too much longer to wait, maybe twenty minutes, before the gang showed up, and I was happy to see them. Jacques was back cracking his stupid jokes, Murray was laughing at everything his friend said, my mom was waving to me, Taylor was smiling about as wide as you could ever smile, and her grandfather looked as determined as he always did.

"Well, there's that young Lance Armstrong," said Jacques in his sort of French accent.

Murray corrected him immediately. "Don't insult the boy like that. He got here without the help of steroids!"

"Kevin, you didn't hear our plan." Taylor was now stopped beside me and taking off her bike helmet. She had a tight green bike shirt on, and she was moving her hand through her dark hair. "After we get to the museum, we're all going to The Hedges."

I shrugged my shoulders. "The what?"

Now my mom was on the other side of me. "In the pamphlet, it says The Hedges are open for any bikers to go swimming and canoeing."

"What's The Hedges?" I was still very confused.

Taylor was now getting off her bike and leaning it up against a tree. "It's one of those old Adirondack camps on Blue Mountain Lake. Some Civil War general owned it."

"It's only a few miles from the museum, and we can either bike there or take a shuttle," said Murray as he stepped off his bike and looked for a place to lean it.

My mom was now taking off her bike helmet. "We figured we'd get to the museum, put up our tents, get our bags and our bathing suits, and then take an easy bike ride over to The Hedges. It's about two miles away. Jacques has a backpack that he's offered can hold all our bathing suits."

"What would you Americans do without me?" he said with a laugh.

Just the idea of getting to spend some time with Taylor seemed pretty exciting, even if she wasn't my girlfriend. And to get to see her in a bathing suit, but I forced myself to not go there. I don't want to be one of those creepy guys!

CHAPTER 5

THE HEDGES

The ten-mile ride to the Adirondack Museum was a lot easier than my earlier race to Long Lake. We must have been going about 14 or 15 miles an hour, and there was a lot of talking and laughing, and we stopped every so often to take some pictures, to drink some water, look at the trees, and the mountains and the white puffy clouds. Sometimes I'd be so lost in my daydream I wouldn't hear a question tossed at me. "Earth to Kevin!" Mom again. "I asked you how fast you biked with that man from Virginia."

"Just about twenty miles an hour," I said.

Jacques let out a long whistle. "I guess this must feel very slow to you now, huh? Very pedestrian?"

"I'm surprised I can keep my balance and not fall over," I said, and everyone laughed. It might have been the first time I ever said anything where everyone laughed at what I said and not how badly I said it.

Even Taylor came up alongside me and laughed. "Good one." She gave me a wink.

The most difficult part of that ten-mile ride was the almost straight uphill into the parking lot of the Adirondack Museum, and when we finally got there, we were all gasping and out of breath. We slowly walked over to get our bags from the truck and then find a location to set up camp.

"I can't believe they're letting us set up tents here at the museum," said Taylor's grandfather. "Aren't they afraid we're going to trample things?"

"Well, I guess it's only one night," said Murray, "and we're bikers, not a marauding army out to pillage and plunder."

"What do you mean we're not going to pillage and plunder? That's the only reason I came on this stupid bike tour," Jacques said, and began laughing.

My mom shook her head and smiled. "You Canadians are too nice to ever pillage."

Jacques bowed to her. "That is true, mademoiselle, but we do like to claim the spoils of war."

We set up our tents behind the art galleries and the office building. We were near the little old schoolhouse I used to think was so cool when I was a kid. My third time setting up the tent, and I was really figuring it out. I could do it in half the time from day one. All the guys had decided to wear their bathing suits and just bike to The Hedges, but my mom and Taylor were going to bring their suits in Jacques' backpack.

The short ride to The Hedges wasn't very comfortable, and I could now understand the importance of wearing those skintight but fanny-padded bike shorts. After two days of riding, I was also getting some butt chafing, a very stiff neck and my wrists were sore. A few other people were also biking along with us, and we were even passed once by the shuttle from the Adirondack Museum, which beeped as it went by. Almost every seat was filled, and the bikers looking out the windows mostly waved to us or gave us a thumbs up. The little town of Blue Mountain Lake was sort of old-looking with some antique stores, an arts center, and a few places to eat. Some of the other bikers stopped to check out the town, but we kept going.

Entering The Hedges was like going back in time. There were big old trees by the side of the road and about ten or fifteen lakeside cabins all decorated with tree branches. There was also a main lodge, a stone lodge, a dining room, and a boathouse. The boathouse had something like twenty canoes and kayaks, and the best part of all was that our bike tour was the only group allowed in that day. We had the place to ourselves.

We placed our bikes by the main lodge and leaned them up against trees or benches—anything we could find. Murray leaned his against a large rock.

"So we can eat here and go swimming and take a kayak or canoe ride?" asked Taylor.

"That's what was written in the pamphlet," said her grandfather, "and I don't see anyone here except the bikers."

"I guess they're really trying to get people excited about coming up to the Adirondacks," said my mom. "It's obviously a public relations move to treat us so special, but I don't mind."

We walked out on the long dock that went far into Blue Mountain Lake. It was a big lake encircled by mountains, with twenty or thirty islands scattered everywhere. There were a few motorboats going up and down the lake, but it was a little after noon in the middle of summer, making it too hot for too many boaters to be out and about. Other than the slight drone of the motorboats, the only other noise was the water lapping at the dock and a few birds chirping away.

"Welcome, bikers, to The Hedges." An older woman with white gray hair was walking toward us. She wore a green shirt that said *The Hedges* on it.

We all turned around and smiled.

"My name is Pat Benton, and I'm the owner here. Have been for the past ten years. My husband, Rip, and I bought the old place and boy, did it need some work, but we put money into it because we felt it was a little piece of heaven."

We all introduced ourselves, and the men all shook

her hand. She wanted to know where we were from and why we were doing the bike ride.

"My husband enjoyed biking," she said.

"So, does your husband bike anymore?" my Mom asked.

"Oh, no, my husband died shortly after we bought the property. Poor dear, he would have loved how this place turned out. But when I heard about this Adirondack Bike Tour, well, I knew he would want me to open it up to all of you, and that's just what I've done. Now we're going to have a cookout by the beach over there after 2:00 p.m., and you may use all the kayaks and canoes that you want—just sign them out by the boathouse with Roger. You can use the entire property till 7:00 p.m. That's when the last shuttle will take everyone back."

"We biked over," I said.

"Oh, well, you can leave a little later then. There are bathrooms in all the dining rooms and the stone lodge. By the beach there, we have many towels you can sign out. Now you have a perfect day to enjoy our lovely lake. I have fliers I want all of you to go home with, and please come back to visit us. We're open year-round. I must get going. It was nice to meet all of you, and I'll be around all day if you have any questions."

We all nodded goodbye and waved to her. "That woman has a bit of energy," said Jacques. "If her husband tried to keep up with her, that might explain why he's no longer here."

My mom gave him a soft punch in the arm. "You're a horrible person," she said.

"Yes, I am."

"I'm going to put my bathing suit on," said Taylor, and she began to walk down the dock.

"I'll join you," said my mom.

My heart began beating faster, the same way it does a few minutes before a big race. The next time I'd see Taylor she'd be in a bathing suit.

"Kevin, I'll meet you at the beach. Get two towels." Taylor said this with a quick look over her shoulder.

"You better go, boy," laughed Jacques.

Taylor's grandfather just sort of glared at me.

I could tell my face was getting red, and my stomach was sort of spinning around. I was about to spend a day at a lake in the Adirondack Mountains with an absolutely gorgeous girl, and she wanted me to get two towels. Maybe I could get a picture of the two of us, and I could post it on Facebook and Instagram, and the guys on the team would see it.

We all walked toward the small beach. There were already a few people out swimming, and a few more paddling around in canoes or kayaks. I really didn't know what to do at a lake. We're not a big swimming family. We often went to Cape Cod and swam at the ocean, but that was mostly riding waves, reading books, and throwing the Frisbee around. But lakes? This was a whole new thing for me. I've never been a big fan of stepping into a lake and not knowing what's at the bottom. There could be rocks or tree stumps, and many of these Adirondack lakes have leeches and snapping turtles. The ocean never bothered me as much. The bottom might have some shells, but because of the waves it was usually smooth on your feet, and where my family swam, the water was too cold for any sharks or jellyfish.

We gathered a few green Adirondack chairs on the beach, and Taylor's grandfather placed a towel on the back of one and then immediately tore off his white cotton shirt and ran down the short beach to the water and dove in. How could he do such a thing? I would be so worried about stepping on something and puncturing my foot. As a runner, my feet are very important to me.

He shot through the water like a missile from a submarine, and when he finally surfaced he was on his back. He threw his head back, sprayed out water. and let out a loud gasp. "This is great!" His grey chest hair matched some of the grey stubble of his beard.

Murray and Jacques also took off their shirts and went out into the water. Murray was a bit more tentative. As he walked in, I could tell he was looking at the water to make sure he didn't step on anything. But Jacques copied Mr. McCabe and ran into the water and did his own dive, mostly a belly flop that splashed water everywhere.

"Come on in, kid," he yelled back at me, water dripping down his face. With his shirt off, I could tell he was in pretty good shape for a guy over forty years old.

I've always been self-conscious about taking my shirt off in public. In my basketball playing days, I hated when we'd play shirts and skins. If I had to take off my shirt, it ruined my entire game. I have bony shoulders. and my elbows are like sharp spears. The elbows can be valuable when I'm in the middle of a big race and trying to fight my way through a crowd, but in real life, they don't look so good. I also have about five hairs on my chest, long straggly black hairs like you might find on a pig, and because I never take my shirt off, I usually get one of those weird tans where the lower two-thirds of my arms are bronzed, but my upper arms and chest are completely white. Still, I took off my shirt and walked toward the water.

The Adirondack air felt cold on my naked chest and shoulders. Because I'm skinny, I'm one of those people who feel cold most of the time, and here I was walking down the beach getting colder with each step, and then I would be getting into the even colder Blue Mountain Lake. The only reason I was doing this was because all the guys were already in the water. Well, Murray was only standing there about knee deep, but the other two were flopping around like a couple of dolphins. Based on Murray's reaction, I knew I'd better get in there and get adjusted before Taylor showed up so I didn't look like a wimp in front of her.

I stepped into the water, and it felt like walking into an ice cream bowl.

"Exhilarating, isn't it?" said Murray.

I knew I was grimacing. "Probably not the word I'd use."

"Kid, you gotta just jump right in." Jacques was now floating on his back. "Murray, show him how it's done. Be a Canadian!"

Murray shrugged, and with a slight groan, jumped out into the water. He didn't go under—he just floated away on his stomach and let out a few sighs.

"Now it's your turn," said Jacques.

I've always hated peer pressure. I suspect it's something that kids and teenagers have to face more than adults, and it's one reason why being an adult one day might not be so bad, even if I did have to suffer through wine and cheese parties. What I really wanted to do was go back to the Adirondack chair, put my shirt on, and sit in the sun to warm up and wait for Taylor to walk out in her bathing suit, but here I was beginning to shiver and I wasn't even shin deep in this chilly Adirondack lake with three old guys taunting me to jump in and become even colder.

"Do we have to count down from ten?"

A few other people on the beach now noticed what was going on. I've always hated any kind of a scene, and here I was being watched by all these people who wanted to see if I was actually going to jump into the cold water. I told Jacques he didn't need to begin a countdown, but somebody else on the beach, another biker I didn't know, started yelling, "Ten, nine, eight," and then I took a deep breath and jumped out into the water.

Bubbles, the sound of water, and cold spray engulfed me. The cold did indeed feel very good. My hair was soaked and my shoulders and stiff neck felt cool and relaxed for the first time in days. I floated around fearing what the bottom might feel like and hoping to not encounter any leeches, slugs, or snapping turtles. I dove underwater and felt the cold devour my entire body. Yes, this was a wonderful thing. I even tried to stand, my toes scrunching the mostly sandy bottom. There were no tree branches, pointy sticks, or biting fish of any kind.

"Well, I see the boys didn't wait for us."

I turned in the direction of Taylor's voice. Water dripped down my face, and looking into the bright sun gave off a kaleidoscope effect. I could hear Taylor and my mom speaking quietly, but with all that water, where was she? She began to gradually come in to focus. Was that her? And why did she seem to look less fit than I would have thought? "I'm over here," she said to the left of where I was looking.

When I got all the water out of my eyes I realized I had been focusing on an older biker lady, but to the left of that woman was Taylor. She was wearing a yellow two-piece bathing suit, I guess it was a bikini, and she was sparkling in the sun. I brushed the water away from my eyes. "The water's great," I said. "Come on in." My heart was rapidly beating away in my chest like it might explode.

She jogged gracefully into the water and then dove,

barely making a splash. When she resurfaced, she was about ten feet away from me far out into the deeper part of the lake. I could tell immediately that she was a much better swimmer than me, but that description would fit perhaps 98% of the world's population. I was a sprint swimmer, one of the fastest swimmers in the world from one part of a built-in backyard swimming pool to the next. I swam like an Olympic champion 100-meter runner with a burst of speed, my arms moving like a race-car engine and my legs kicking away like a high-speed helicopter, but after thirty or forty yards I usually had nothing left.

"This water's cold," said my mom, who was now standing ankle-deep in the water. She wore a black one-piece bathing suit that I had never seen before. In fact, it looked new. Why would she buy a new bathing suit for this bike tour?

"You Americans don't know what cold water is. Isn't that right, Murray?"

"That's right," said Murray, through chattering teeth. He had goose bumps on his white scraggly arms.

I didn't really know what to do in lake water. In Cape Cod, I would just ride the waves up and down, sometimes I'd float on my back and sometimes on my stomach. I would catch a wave and ride it as far in to the beach as possible, but there were no waves in Blue Mountain Lake, so I just sort of floated around and swam a little. It was refreshing and all, but pretty boring.

"Kevin, are you a good swimmer?" Taylor yelled to me. She was even deeper and farther away than a few minutes before.

"I'm okay," I said, floating on my back. "I do most of my swimming at the ocean. I like to ride waves."

My mom was now swimming in my direction, with Jacques swimming toward her.

"Looks like they're serving lunch by the beach," said Murray. He might have been as bored as I was, or desperate to get something in his stomach to get warm.

The smell of hotdogs and hamburgers wafted in from the grill, and that aroma sort of jumpstarted my hunger.

"Kevin, come on out." Taylor was floating around about thirty yards away from me. She seemed to be a natural in cold Adirondack lakes.

There was no rope, no big rock or raft to hang on to, but I knew I would have to try and swim out there. Here was a beautiful girl in a yellow bathing suit asking me to join her in a swim. If I died getting there, it would have been a pretty romantic way to go. Wasn't there some poet—Lord Byron or Percy Shelly, one of those English poets—that drowned in a lake? If I died swimming out to Taylor I'd be a hero to my friends. At least Dipper anyway. Maybe someone would one day write a romantic poem about me. Maybe Taylor would honor me by naming her first son Kevin.

I began swimming in her direction.

"Take your time, Kevin. You're not in a backyard pool." It was my mom embarrassing me by giving advice, even though it was advice I needed to hear.

I tried to take my time and not sprint to Taylor. I tried to move my head in the opposite direction as I moved my arms, the way I've seen all the good swimmers move. I tried to take a few breaths, but mostly I was sucking in water. I could see that I was getting closer and closer to her, but I was also getting much more tired. It was a beautiful day in a gorgeous lake in the middle of the summer and I really didn't want to ruin everyone's day by drowning just when people were arriving at The Hedges and lunch was about to be served.

"You made it." It was Taylor, and she was right—I was floating alongside her. Maybe I was a pretty good swimmer after all. I was going to say something, but I was trying to control my breathing before I spoke.

"Look at all those mountains. And those islands. And look at how pretty The Hedges is." Taylor spun around in the water without a care in the world looking at the greens and blues all around us.

I was just trying to stay afloat. "It's pretty."

There were mountains and islands and water and blue sky, but I was really looking mostly at Taylor.

Jacques and my mom were now swimming toward us. I figured that was probably good because if I began to go down, there were now three people who could save me.

"I'm going to eat," said Murray from far away as he walked out of the water. People were lining up at the charcoal pit where the food was being cooked.

"Hey, you're swimming pretty well." My mom was now floating right next to me. Her brown eyes were bright and full. I hadn't seen them like that in a long time.

The three of us floated in a circle, but I knew I couldn't sustain this for much longer. "I'm hungry, too," I gasped.

"You Americans are always hungry for food, for power, for everything."

My mom said some snarky comment back to him, but I began swimming away toward shallow water. I didn't want to panic, but I knew I could only stay afloat for maybe another minute or so, and then I was going down. I began my sprint with my face in the water and kicked my legs with all the power I had, and helicoptering my arms as fast as they could go. I probably looked like some sort of beached whale moving in to shore, but at least I would be standing on ground with my head above water and not at the bottom of the lake sucking it in. After a few seconds I slowed down, took my face out of the water, and slowly moved my legs to the ground. Yes, my toes and then my entire foot landed on solid earth. I stood and took a deep breath.

"I'm gonna get some food before you." Taylor raced past me on her way to the shore. I was content to watch her swim steadily by me and then gracefully walk on the beach as rivulets of water trickled down her strong back and muscular legs.

After we dried off, we got in line for food, and then took our plates and our lemonade down to the Adirondack chairs on the beach. I put my shirt on as fast as I could because I was still too embarrassed for anyone to see how skinny I was, but Taylor sat there in that wonderful yellow bathing suit as comfortable as can be, leaning back in that chair, eating and laughing with everyone else. I have been raised to see a woman as a human being who is the equal of any man and not as an object to be stared at, but I sure wanted to spend all day staring at her

My mom was sitting the same way between Jacques and Murray, like she was the Queen of the Adirondacks. She held her food plate gracefully atop her chest, a long leg curled one on top of the other in front of her. If she needed something from the food table, Jacques would jump up and get it. I began to wonder if I was looking at Taylor the same way he looked at my mom.

"After we eat, let's all go for a kayak ride." Taylor smiled and shook her head like a puppy dog trying to get some cheese.

And that's what we did. We signed out six kayaks from the boathouse, and as a flotilla, we paddled away.

It took me a few minutes to get the hang of a kayak, but once I did, I liked the feel of it cutting quietly through the water. Unlike a canoe, a kayak puts you much closer to the water, so you feel like you're part of the lake. I paddled next to Taylor, who seemed to really know what she was doing. "You've done a lot of this, haven't you?"

She smiled. "My grandfather and I have our own kayaks, and during the summer we sometimes get out on the water one or two times a month."

It was beginning to sound like she and her grandfather did just about everything together.

Jacques was blabbing on and on, and I really just wanted to get away with Taylor. I'm not a kayak veteran or anything, but it seems to me that it should be something that's done quietly, like putting for a birdie in golf. "Hey, let's go over to that big island out there and explore it." I said this only to Taylor as everyone else seemed interested in Jacques' latest funny story about the last time he was kayaking in the Canadian wilderness.

"I'd like that," said Taylor. And then she raised her voice for everyone else. She had such a perfect voice, the kind you hear on radio or TV commercials. "Kevin and I are going to kayak over by that island," and she motioned where it was with her paddle.

Jacques made these strange sounds, and then he said, "Sure, why don't you get away from the old people. We understand, don't we?"

My mom gave him a nasty look. "Have a good time," she said, and then she smiled at the two of us.

"Don't make me nervous," said her grandfather, and he was looking directly at me.

It felt nice to break away from the other four, but I could tell Taylor's grandfather kept watching us as we paddled away. They sure seemed to have a strong relationship. "Finally, it's quiet again." Taylor and I were paddling right next to each other. The only sounds were our paddles in the water and our breathing. We could still hear Jacques in the distance telling some story as the four of them continued up the lake. My God how that man could talk. We were now almost in the center of the lake.

"That Jacques is a lively one," she said.

"Did you ever notice that most distance runners are sort of quiet?" I said.

"I have," said Taylor. "I guess it has to do with why we like to go for long runs alone."

"Some people like to listen to music when they run, but I like to look around and listen, kind of pay attention to what's around me."

"I'm the same way," said Taylor, "and I hate running on a treadmill."

"Me, too."

We paddled in silence for a few minutes, enjoying the warm sun on us, the rhythm of the paddling, and the splashing of the water. I tried to sneak a few glances at Taylor as she paddled. I had never been alone with a girl my age for this long, and I loved how athletic she was and how comfortable she seemed in her own body. I wish I felt as comfortable in my own gangly physique.

"It sounds like you and your grandfather do a lot, but I never hear about your parents. They must be athletic kind of people, too?"

There was an uncomfortable pause and then Taylor said, "They were very athletic. I guess no one brought this up yet, but my parents died in a car crash three years ago. I live with my grandfather now."

I stopped paddling and felt like jumping into the water and racing away never to be seen again. How could I have ever been so stupid to ask about her parents? It's no wonder I've never had a girlfriend. I don't know how to have a normal conversation with anyone. "I'm so sorry."

Taylor moved her kayak next to mine. "Don't feel sorry. You didn't do anything wrong. It's kind of hard to ease that into a normal discussion. My parents were the best. We did everything together. One of the few times they were getting away by themselves, a cross-country ski weekend in Vermont, and they were killed by a drunk driver on the Northway. It was a front page story in the newspaper for a day or two and on the local news. Usually people bring it up, and I was kind of surprised no one did."

"Leave it to me." I just sat there in the kayak with my mouth open, in shock. "I'm so sorry."

Taylor smiled. "I know, but I'm lucky to have such a great grandfather. He's like another father to me now. I was in bad shape after the accident. Didn't want to do anything. Didn't want to go to school. Never called my friends. I was depressed. My grandfather had me see a therapist, and she said I needed to join a club or a sport; something. So, I joined cross country, and that was the best thing I ever did in my life. All my friends are on the team. Those girls saved me. It kind of saved my grandfather, too. He was as depressed as me. It was his daughter who had died. So I started running and he started biking with me. We got into hiking, bought kayaks. I guess all that moving kept us going."

We were just floating around on the lake. I wanted to reach out and take her hand. I wanted to put my arms around her and hug the sadness out of her, but she didn't seem so sad. Her parents died three years ago, and she seemed happier than I was. How could that be?

Taylor smiled. "You would have liked my parents."

"I already like them. That's great that your grandfather bikes with you."

"When you're a black girl it's not such a good idea to run alone."

"Really." I had never thought of that. Running alone was one of my favorite things to do. Running by myself I could tune things out and just get into the rhythm of the run, the sound of my breathing, the feel of my feet hitting the gravel in the road and the pumping of my heart.

"There are some neighborhoods in the city my grandfather and I would never run or bike through."

"Oh?"

Taylor gave me a perplexed look. "I guess you being a white teenage boy, it would never occur to you. You're welcome everywhere, but it's not like that when you're black."

I knew there was racism and I remembered that horrible George Floyd murder and the Black Lives Matter protests, but racism here where I live? She was right, I guess. As a white boy I took so much for granted. What did I know about racism. I went to a pretty much all-white public school in the suburbs. I didn't really know any black people, and I lived in a suburban neighborhood with very little diversity.

"Sometimes I wonder if my parents were alive, would I still be a runner?" Taylor began paddling again. "Let's go jump off that rock cliff." She nodded in the direction of the big island ahead of us.

Here we go again, I thought. It was hard enough to swim into the deep water, but now we were going to jump off a cliff that was twenty, maybe twenty-five-feet high. We'd be jumping in the deep water. Then it hit me. Maybe that was my way out. "We better check to see if the water's deep enough."

"It's deep enough," she said. She was already at

the island, stepping out of her boat, and pulling her kayak up on the shore between two big boulders. She seemed fearless. I bet she was never afraid to go out to fast in a race like I was.

"I'll stay out here in the water and watch you jump." I was now floating around in the general area where she would soon be landing. The water was deep enough, but she needed to jump out pretty far to get to the deep water and not land on any big rocks below.

She almost ran up the trail that took her to the top of the rock. How could she do that in bare feet?

"Wow! It's a lot higher up here than you think." She stood on the highest part of the cliff and looked around. "It's pretty up here, and you can see far away. I hope my grandfather isn't watching."

"You don't have to jump," I said. She's the one that looked pretty up there on that rock, and I was worried that she'd land badly and break one of those perfect legs of hers. How could I even get her out of the water if she became unconscious? But before I could say anything else, she took a leap, pinching her nose with her right thumb and pointer finger, and soared away and down into the cold Adirondack lake.

She sprang up almost immediately. "Yes!" She pumped her fist a few times and swam toward my kayak. When she got to my boat she held on and said, "Now it's your turn." She was adjusting the top and bottom of her bathing suit as she spoke to me.

There have been a few times in my life when I

forced myself to do something I really didn't want to do. When I was cut from the ninth-grade basketball team, I was depressed and felt like a complete loser, but for some reason, I wanted to join something, a club, a sport; something. So, I signed up for the indoor track team. I forced myself to walk into that classroom where the first meeting was being held. There were forty boys I didn't know sitting around and talking, and they all got quiet when I entered. But I didn't run out of that room, as much as I wanted to. I stayed for the meeting, put my name down, and joined that team. Now was another one of those times. I didn't want to jump off that rock in any way, but I was going to do it. I needed to push myself. That, and Taylor was watching. This girl who had lost her parents three years ago and who could not run in certain neighborhoods because she was black. What choice did I have? "All right, it's my turn."

Taylor pushed herself away from my kayak and swam back toward her boat which was beached on the other side of the island. I waited for her to pull herself up on the rocks, then get into her kayak and push off. I then moved into the position where she had been. I almost fell about five times trying to get out of the kayak, but eventually I was standing on the rocks that were covered with duck poop. It was so gross, but if Taylor could do this, then so could I.

"Just follow that trail up to the top." Taylor was back in her kayak now floating just off shore. "Hey, throw me your shirt."

I was planning on jumping in my shirt mostly because I hated taking my shirt off. "My white skin is going to blind you," I said as I slipped the shirt over my head.

"I have my sunglasses on," said Taylor and she caught the shirt as I tossed it to her. "And you look nice without your shirt on."

I couldn't believe she said that. If I died on this jump, then I was going to die with a smile on my face. Taylor said I looked good with my shirt off. Although my feet hurt with every step, sharp rocks, sticks, pebbles and hot sand, I still made it all the way to the top. It was indeed very high at the top. I could see Taylor far below in her kayak. I could just barely make out where The Hedges was, far away and to my right, and I thought I saw four kayaks even farther away from there. They looked like little toy kayaks floating on a distant lake.

"Remember to jump out, and I'll get my kayak over to you as fast as I can."

I felt a breeze high up where I was, and if this was going to be the last thing I'd ever see, then that would be okay. I wanted to yell out, "Taylor, I love you," but instead I just jumped out as far as I could and sank into the water like a bowling ball. It was an eruption of sound as I crashed, and white bubbles were everywhere, but it was also about the most thrilling thing I had ever done. When I finally emerged from the water, there she was only a few feet away with her kayak. I reached out for the boat. She smiled and clapped. "You did it."

"I did it."

CHAPTER 6

We took a few more jumps, and then decided to just beach our kayaks and sit under the shade of a tree on the island. Taylor had brought along her water bottle, and she even let me drink from it. I thought that was a pretty good sign about how close we had gotten in the last few days.

"You don't normally do stuff like that, do you?" We were both leaning our backs against a tree trunk. Her right leg was bent straight up; her left leg slightly brushing against my right leg. It was so intimate I wanted to scream out in joy about how much I loved the world.

"Oh, sure, I jump off twenty-foot cliffs just about every week." We both laughed. "Was it that obvious?"

Taylor smiled and looked me directly in the eyes. I've always been wary of looking anyone directly in the eyes. "That's one of the things I like most about you. So many other boys always try to be so macho and prove how tough they are. It's like they're always trying to act like they know everything. Why can't they just admit they don't? I could tell just watching you put up your tent and take it down that you didn't know what you were doing and that was okay."

"I don't think boys have fully evolved yet," I said and we both laughed again. "Was it that obvious with the tent? I thought I was doing pretty good."

Taylor smiled. "It was pretty obvious. You're almost like one of my girlfriends, and even though we haven't known each other for that long, I feel like I can tell you just about anything."

Well, I wasn't so happy to hear her say that—at least that first part. I was beginning to wonder if she thought I was gay. "So, try me out. Tell me something you'd tell your girlfriends."

She took a sip from her water bottle and looked up at the big fluffy sky above. "Well, I don't want to embarrass you and talk about boys, which is what my girlfriends and I talk about a lot, but I sometimes tell them things I'm worried about, like how overprotective my grandfather is."

I realized a long time ago that I'm not much of a talker, but I like listening, so when she said that I just sat there nodding my head and waiting for her to continue.

"He already lost his youngest daughter, my mom, and I know he's always worried about losing me. He's always talking about how we live in such a racist society, how there's systemic racism in America."

I had heard talk like that before in school, especially when we read books by African-American writers, but I never had a black friend before who actually talked about this stuff. "Do you think we live in a racist society?"

Taylor smiled. "Of course, but don't get me going. All you need are eyes to notice there are no other people with my skin color on this trip."

"I guess you're right," I said. I didn't want to tell her there were very few Black people even in my suburban high school. "Your grandfather doesn't seem like an angry guy to me."

"My Grandpop is the best," said Taylor, "but his wife, my Grandma, died about ten years ago, and his other daughter lives in New Mexico, so I'm pretty much all he has left. It can be a bit stifling. Why do you think I wanted to get away on our kayak, and why do you think I was so excited to find you on this bike ride?"

That comment hurt a bit. "I thought you were happy to see me because I'm a runner like you." I said this with a smile, but my insides were a little fluttery.

Taylor sat straight up like she had received an electrical shock. "Oh, of course, I was excited that you were a runner. That didn't come out right. That sounded horrible. I like you for who you are. You're gentle, and I can tell you're kind."

This was getting embarrassing, which is one reason why I hate heart-to-heart talks, not that I've had too many of them. "I know what you mean," I said, even though I was still a bit lost.

"I couldn't imagine anyone I'd rather be with on this bike ride than you." The way she said that, I believed her. "So, what do you talk about with your friends?"

I couldn't tell her that I didn't really have any friends. Dipper was sort of a friend, but we never had any deep talks or anything. "We talk about running. We talk about our splits for the 1600-meter run. We mostly just make fun of each other."

Taylor laughed. "You must talk about girls."

On our long runs, I've overheard the guys say some gross things about what they'd do with certain girls in our school or girls on our team, but I never joined in. "Sometimes we talk about girls. How they look, stuff like that."

Taylor was now laughing. "Yeah, I bet you talk about girls. That's one reason why my grandfather wanted me to go to an all-girls high school—to keep me away from those 'hormonal boys,' as he calls them."

"Those hormones help us run fast," I said, breaking into a smile.

We then talked about some of our favorite things, what we like to eat, and what music we listen to. We both liked the song 'Long May You Run' by that old guy Neil Young. I could have listened to that melodic voice of hers all day, but after a while we just sat there in silence for a few seconds. It was quiet on this island. There were a few birds calling, and the waves were crashing softly on the rocks, but it was mostly just peaceful. In the movies, the guy would reach his hand out or look directly into the beautiful girl's eyes and tell her how much he loved her. She would lean in toward him and they would have a passionate kiss, and the camera would pan to a bird calling or a wave crashing on a rock and the audience would be left to wonder what happened next.

"So, I told you a sort of secret about me and my grandfather. Tell me something no one knows about you."

"I'm scared my parents are gonna split up." It just erupted out of my mouth before I was able to clamp it down. It was something I had never spoken aloud.

Taylor didn't react alarmingly in any way. "Why is that?"

I moved my hand as if to brush it away. "Oh, you don't want to hear the whole story."

"Yes, I do." And then she stopped leaning against the tree and moved around to face me directly.

"My dad seems to care more about his job than us. He's a federal prosecutor. He's always at work. He gets his name in the newspaper all the time, and he gets interviewed on the local news sometimes. He's good at what he does, but he's not a very good husband or father anymore."

"That's so sad." Taylor nodded her head as she patted me on my shoulder.

My voice changed and my eyes got a bit watery, but I fought to keep my emotions in check. I'm very good at keeping my emotions in check. "It wasn't always that way. We used to go on vacations and bike rides and hike and have fun and laugh. We even tried to get him to go on this bike ride."

"Have you told him this? How you want him back?"

I shrugged. "All the time, but it doesn't seem to matter."

We sat there in silence. Neither of us knew where to go with this. "Well, I guess people can fall out of love. Things get in the way of relationships."

"I guess." I wanted to tell her that if she and I were together, I'd never let anything get in the way of our love.

"Maybe if they separated for a while, they'd realize how much they love each other."

"Maybe." I wasn't enjoying this talk anymore. That was another problem about having a real conversation. It sometimes ruins the mood.

"I'm glad your mom came on this trip, and I'm glad she brought you. A lot of people in that situation would probably just sit around and get bitter, but she's doing things even if he's not willing to do them."

"Yeah, my mom's pretty cool."

"She's a regular hipster," said Taylor, and we both laughed. "Let's take one more look off the cliff, and then I guess we should head back to The Hedges. I'm feeling a little dehydrated."

We were both a bit sore getting back up on our feet after all the biking and kayaking and jumping off the cliff. I let Taylor go on the trail ahead of me.

When we got to the top of the rock, it was great to take in the view one last time. The sun was moving farther down toward the horizon, and it seemed to sparkle even more than before on the lake. There was a mother duck and her ducklings swimming around in the water below us, and the breeze felt cool in the warm sun. "There's not much better than summer in the Adirondacks," I said, standing next to Taylor.

"Winter in the Adirondacks is pretty nice, too," she said.

"I also like the fall." I was smiling and feeling so happy at that moment.

"But the spring is horrible."

"You got that right," I said. "All that mud. Yuck." There were a few kayaks on the lake, mostly in the vicinity of The Hedges. "When we leave this island, we're going to miss all this quiet."

"Yeah, we will. Thanks for a great afternoon." And then Taylor reached up and gave me a peck on the cheek.

I almost fell off the cliff. Yes, it was a peck, but a peck from a girl who looked like Taylor counted much more than a kiss from most of the girls in the world. It was a peck a sister might give a brother, but it was better than a high-five or a fist bump. I knew I was smiling, and I tried to control the smile, so I took one last look at the lake. About four hundred yards to my left two kayaks emerged from behind another island. The people looked small, and I could barely make them out as they stepped out of their boats. My faraway vision has never been good, which makes it hard for me to pick out the finish line in most cross-country races. They looked like a man and a woman, but it was hard to see for sure. They helped balance each other as they stepped out of their boats and onto the island. I wondered if they were also from the bike ride and were exploring islands the way Taylor and I had. Maybe there was a cliff on the other side, and they were going to jump. As they walked across the beach, they immediately went in to a strong embrace with their arms wrapped tightly around each other. I knew I should look away, but I began to feel a slight sweat breaking out on my forehead. It was their bathing suits. The woman wore a black one-piece suit and the man wore one of those brightly colored Hawaiian suits. My hands began to shake.

"Are you coming, or do I have to kayak back alone?" Taylor was climbing into her boat down below me.

"I'm coming," I said, turning my eyes away from that island and telling myself that a lot of people wear black bathing suits and flowery Hawaiian suits.

But how many were on Blue Mountain Lake today?

The fifteen-minute paddle back to The Hedges seemed to take forever. Taylor talked about how hungry she was and how nice it would be to have something cold to drink, and I kept telling myself we'd pull up at the boathouse and see Jacques telling jokes to everyone on the beach and my mom waving from her Adirondack chair. I also wondered if maybe I should go back to that island and confront them, but what if it wasn't them? Maybe I should tell Taylor what I thought I saw. If it was my mom and Jacques, maybe the whole thing was just a little innocent sort of hug—but it sure didn't look innocent to me. It was the kind of hug I wanted to give Taylor every day for the rest of my life.

As we got closer to The Hedges, I searched the beach and the Adirondack chairs. *Please let them be there*, I thought. *Please don't let this be what I think it might be.*

"You were beginning to make me nervous," said Taylor's grandfather from the Adirondack chair where he had eaten his lunch earlier. When he said that he was staring only at me.

"But we're still missing two of them," said Murray, seated next to him and drinking from a can of beer.

At that moment I hated my dad. This was all his fault. He should have been on this trip.

"I wonder where your mom is," said Taylor.

I just shrugged my shoulders. "I guess we should sign these back in." I steered my kayak over to the boathouse. My hands were shaking, and I could feel something moving up my throat.

It was a half hour later when we saw the two red kayaks slowly moving in our direction from the other side of the lake. "They are gonna be sore after paddling for that long," said Murray.

The two of them paddled side by side, talking and laughing. I wanted to throw up right there on the beach.

"I thought we were going to have to bike back without you," said Murray as they came closer to shore.

The two of them were all smiles and waving to us, and I just sat there staring straight ahead, over their heads, wishing this trip was over.

CHAPTER 7

DAY 3: BLUE MOUNTAIN LAKE
TO WARRENSBURG (48 MILES)

I tried to smile when they arrived back at the beach. I really did, but my mom knew something was up right away. I guess she knows me a little too well. I thought I knew her pretty well. I guess I was wrong.

"Are you okay, Kevin?" She was all smiles when she arrived at our chairs on the beach, brushing her long hair off her shoulders and adjusting her bathing suit top.

"We jumped off a cliff from one of the islands," said Taylor, drinking a can of iced tea.

My mom kept staring at me. "You jumped off a cliff?"

I nodded and took a sip from my Gatorade.

"He jumped four times, Mrs. Walsh."

My mom shook her head in amazement. "Four times."

"Just trying something new," I said, wondering how sarcastic I sounded. Wondering if my tone sounded accusatory. "So, where were you?" I knew I sounded like the parent asking the child why they came home late from the high-school dance, but it was too late to take it back.

"Jacques and I wanted to explore some islands and see the other side of the lake."

"We were actually bored with all Murray's stories and gave him the slip," said Jacques as he pulled a chair over for my mom to sit on. When was the last time I saw my father do something like that?

"Now that's a lie," said Murray. "When you're around, no one is ever able to tell a story because they can't get a word in. For the peace and quiet of being alone I would have let you give me the slip."

The three of them were all laughing, but I could sense that Taylor's grandfather was also getting a bit tired of The Jacques and Murray Show.

We hung around at The Hedges for another hour or so. I tried to be friendly and sociable, but part of me wanted to blurt out, "Why were the two of you hugging each other on the island, and what else did you do?" But I hate scenes, so I just sat there sipping my drink and sometimes speaking about stuff that didn't matter much to me anymore. What I was really thinking about was what my life was going to be like in the next few months. Would my parents split up? Would I have to do that horrible shuffle from one parent to another? Would I be able to stay in my own bedroom in my own house? Would I have to have breakfast four mornings a week with Jacques sitting across the table from me blabbing away in his French/Canadian accent? I wanted to put my running shoes on and run as far and as fast as I could.

◉

We were all pretty tired on the two-mile ride back to the Adirondack Museum. Once again we had to climb that killer hill, and none of us had much left after being out in the sun all afternoon. I took a shower in the truck when I got back, and I didn't even care who was in there. I was sort of sleepwalking with everything I did.

We had a lasagna dinner in the auditorium at the museum. I ate only because I knew I needed to eat something, but it pretty much tasted like nothing. The six of us sat together as usual for dinner, and I could see how much Jacques and my mom were looking at each other for the entire meal. It made me want to vomit, and if I did, I was going to try to projectile on Jacques.

During dessert—chocolate cake—Taylor turned to me and said quietly, "Let's walk around the museum after we eat. Let's check out that Adirondack Experience exhibit."

I nodded my head. The four adults had also decided to do the same thing, but Taylor pulled me away in the opposite direction so we could talk. We walked toward the *Logging in the Adirondacks* exhibit, and when we were safely away from them she said, "I'm so sorry." She reached out and gently took my hand. Her hands were warm and smooth.

I shrugged. Did she know about my mom and Jacques? "Sorry about what?"

"About what I said to you."

I didn't know what she was talking about. "What you said?"

She let my hand go. "Well, I kind of hinted that I was happy you were here so I wouldn't have to be around my grandfather all the time, and that's not true at all."

I gave her a big smile. Ear to ear. "I know that."

"So you're not mad at me?" she asked.

"Not at all."

"Then why are you acting so sad? I thought we had a great day. I know I did."

I guess I would not be a very good poker player. I guess I let people know my feelings even when I think I'm hiding them. "I think Jacques and my mom have a little thing going."

Taylor just looked at me for a few seconds. "A what?"

I rolled my eyes and stared at some of the big logging saws in front of me. "You know."

"I don't believe that."

I told her about what I saw from the cliff.

"Are you sure it was them?"

"One-hundred percent."

Taylor scratched her head. "Well, I'm sure it's all very innocent. It might have just been a hug. I doubt it was anything else. I mean, you don't think… it was an island… there were boats all around."

"I don't know."

We walked back outside and found a bench that had a nice overlook of Blue Mountain Lake. "What are you gonna do?"

I looked at the islands to figure out which island they had been on. It was impossible to tell. "I don't know. I guess I'll just see how tomorrow goes, and the day after. What do you think I should do?"

Taylor just took hold of my hand and we both stared out at the lake as nightfall quickly approached. It was a bright orange/red color where the sun had just set.

When we got back to our tents, Taylor's grandfather was sitting outside reading with a headlamp on his baseball hat, but the other three were nowhere in sight. It was pretty buggy, and I didn't feel much like socializing, so I said goodnight to the two of them and went inside my tent to read for a few minutes before trying to fall asleep. I read some emails and checked Facebook and Instagram. I didn't feel like responding to anything I saw, but I did send my dad a text about where we were and what we did, and I told him that he should call my mom and check in with her.

I heard my mother and Jacques return very late, long after I had turned my flashlight off. She called my name once quietly, but I just rolled over in my sleeping bag and pretended to be asleep.

The next morning, as my mom and I took down our tents, she leaned over and whispered to me. "I'm getting pretty tired of your moodiness, young man."

"My moodiness, huh?" I said.

My mother quickly folded up her tent poles. "That's two times you just sat there and moped about like a little boy while other people were talking and asking you questions. Maybe you should stop seeing that nice girl. It's ruining your mood, and it's beginning to ruin my time here. I spent quite a bit of money to go on this trip, and I'm having a good time. I don't want you to ruin it."

I just sat there taking down my tent and listening to her whisper how angry she was with me. Part of me wanted to yell at her about what I saw, but it was early morning and most people weren't even up yet. I was going to sit and watch and see how the day played out. And I had Taylor on my side. She'd watch everything, too. There was no need to tip my hand just yet. "Sorry. I was tired, and I don't mean to ruin your time. Yesterday was a lot of fun."

My mom gave a quick smile. "I haven't had that

much fun in a long time. So, please, be more pleasant. I'm sorry Taylor has a boyfriend. She's not married to him, you know, and the two of you are such big runners, and he's a soccer player, who knows? Maybe one day the two of you will be dating, but at least enjoy her friendship with the days we have left."

"I guess even when people are married, that's not such a big deal anymore," I said, and then stuffed my tent into its bag.

"What's that supposed to mean?"

I avoided saying anything more and promised my mother I'd be more friendly and less moody. "Oh, and Taylor is an orphan."

"What?"

I told her what Taylor said to me about her parents and their car accident and how she lives with her grandfather.

"That's terrible," she said.

"So maybe now you can see why I was a bit moody." I knew it was a lousy thing to say and phony as hell, but it just came out of me. More importantly, it worked.

My mom reached over and gave me a hug. "That poor, poor girl. It happened on the Northway? A few years ago? I think I remember that now. A drunk driver? I kind of remember that was big news for a few days. So sad."

We ate breakfast in the Lake View Café, where Murray read about our Day 3 Agenda. Jacques probably would have read it, but he was too busy looking at my mom and joking with her. "We have a lot of downhill today. We're starting at 2,000 feet, and forty-eight miles later we'll be in Warrensburg at a little over 1,000 feet."

"That's my kind of biking day," said Jacques as he stuffed a bagel in his mouth. Everything he did sort of repulsed me now. The way he scratched his nose and put his finger in his ear. And that little French accent was more irritating than appealing, and I didn't like how tight-fitting his shorts and shirts were. He also had these long gray chest hairs that had a way of sticking out of his bike shirts. I don't know why my mom would be the least bit interested in him.

"Our first stop is in Indian Lake at about thirteen miles," continued Murray.

"Shouldn't they rename that town Native American Lake," laughed Jacques. "Isn't that what you Americans are doing now to not offend your native people."

We all just sort of glared at him.

Jacques looked at all of us with a big smile on his face. "Well, that's what I keep reading about in Ottawa."

Taylor's grandfather looked directly at him. "I guess we're all getting a little tired of you making fun of America. I served my country. We're not perfect. I had great-great grandparents who were enslaved. God knows this country is a work in progress, but there's a lot of good that goes on here."

"I agree, James, " said Jacques, holding his hands out in some sort of apology. "I love America. I always root for them in the Olympics."

"We're not a perfect country," continued Taylor's grandfather, "but my ancestors would be happy to see me biking freely through this country now with my granddaughter."

We were all quiet for what felt like a very uncomfortable few seconds until Jacques said, "James, there is not one country without sin, and I respect you and the United States for all you have done."

Taylor's grandfather gave a broad smile. "I will admit that Canada has a much better national anthem than the US."

We all laughed and Jacques said, "Agreed."

Murray stared at Jacques and shook his head. "May I continue?" He then cleared his throat. "From Mile 20 to Mile 24, we'll drop to 900 feet."

"Let's hope our brakes are in good shape," said my mom, who was sitting awfully close to Jacques, but looking over at Taylor during most of this conversation. I knew she was feeling sorry for her.

"At 29 miles, we have another stop at the North Creek train platform," said Murray.

"Isn't that where Teddy Roosevelt was sworn in as President after McKinley was assassinated?" I said. I've always been a bit of a geek about the presidents.

"Not quite, Mr. Kevin Walsh," said Murray, "but that was the train station he rushed to after hiking Mt. Marcy and then getting word about how ill your President McKinley was. This train in North Creek rushed him to Albany." Everyone was quiet and staring at how he was able to know all this. "It says all this in the pamphlet here."

"And then from Albany he took a train to Buffalo," said Taylor's grandfather, "and that's where he was sworn in as the next president."

"He's one of my favorite American presidents," said Jacques. Everyone just blankly looked at him. "I'm just saying, I'm bully on Teddy." My mom was the only one who laughed.

"They have a good coffee shop in North Creek named Sarah's or Sophie's something like that," I said. "Mom, do you remember when we went there with dad after skiing at Gore a few winters ago?" I looked directly at Jacques when I said that.

My mom nodded her head.

"Let's get some lunch there," said Taylor's grandfather. "I'm getting tired of eating granola bars at these rest stops."

"I'm bully on that, too," said Jacques, who then followed Taylor's grandfather to get more coffee. It was obvious he must have felt badly about what he had said earlier, and he shook Mr. McCabe's hand and the two men talked and laughed as they got to the coffee machine.

As usual we made our morning pit stops to the bathroom before getting on our bikes for that day's ride. I was actually getting used to waiting on line for a free toilet. We filled our water bottles and put air in our tires, and I could see how much fun it would be to just live on a bike and go from one place to another. I didn't think about television, or checking my phone for any messages. Even my butt and my neck and wrists were feeling okay, like they wanted to get back on that bike and get moving. The only thing bothering me was this strange vibe between my mom and Jacques, and it was the one thing I had no control over.

As I put my bike pack on, my mom walked over and said, "Did you tell your father to call me today?"

I sort of shrugged. "I don't know. Maybe."

She put her pack on the back of her bike. "He wanted to know if there was something going on. What would he mean by asking that?"

I shrugged again in an, 'I don't know' way.

"What do you think is going on here?"

I love and hate how my mom has the ability to hone right in on something. She's never afraid to ask those tough questions. She would have been a great reporter on that TV show *60 Minutes*. "You just seem to be hanging around with Jacques so much. I don't know. It seems sort of weird."

"And you're hanging with Taylor."

"But I'm not married."

My mom put her right hand on my left shoulder. "Nothing's going on with me and that crazy Canadian. But he's paying attention to me." We were both quiet for a few seconds, and it was about as awkward as I've ever felt in my life. "You're my son, and we don't need to say things we'll both be embarrassed about, but it's important to be noticed."

I knew what she was talking about. I run every day after school with ten or twelve guys on the team right in the middle of the pack, and no one ever says much of anything to me. No one invites me to their house. When they talk about going to a movie, they all make plans, and then they notice that I'm there, too, and that's when they'll sometimes invite me. I'm always the afterthought. I'm like a piece of driftwood just floating along with the tide, and the sad thing is I've grown to expect that, which is why I was so shocked Taylor knew my name and sought me out rather than the other way around. "But he's a bit of a jerk," I said.

My mom was smiling. "I know he's a jerk, but he's treating me like I'm something special. He sees me. He's also hurting very much right now. He lost his job last year and fell into a depression. Murray thought it would be good for him to come on this bike trip to move and to see people and hopefully begin to get his life back in better shape."

Although I wanted to, I couldn't bring myself to

ask what they did on that island. Maybe it was just an innocent hug after all. "How did Dad sound?"

"Worried."

"Maybe that's good," I said. "Maybe he'll start noticing you again."

My mom placed her water bottle in the container beneath her seat. "And maybe this is something your father and I should be discussing—not you and me."

"I went in the back room to get you a blueberry granola bar," said Jacques, who sort of appeared out of nowhere and pushed his bike toward us. "It was the last one, but I know it's your favorite."

My mom looked at me and said quietly, "He notices." And then she turned to him and smiled as she took the granola bar. "Thanks," and she placed it in her pack.

Today's ride would take us down Route 30 and Route 28 going south. The road had a nice shoulder, and the weather was cool, about sixty degrees and a bit breezy. All of us wore light jackets to keep us warm. I could tell we were getting into a more crowded part of the Adirondacks. There were more cars and trucks and houses. We rode single file, and Taylor and I shared the lead for the early part. I loved biking behind her. When I was behind her the miles seemed to just go by with very little effort.

A few miles out of the town of Blue Mountain Lake, we passed a hiking trail that would take you to Tyrell Pond. "Mom," I yelled back, "do you remember that hot day we hiked in to that pond and saw those swimmers?"

"I want to hear this story," said Jacques.

"It was on that trail just there," said my mom pointing to a trail on the left side of the road. "It's part of the Northville-Lake Placid Trail."

"The what?" asked Murray. We were all shouting as we biked and occasionally passing a biker every so often by yelling out an "On your left."

"It's a trail that goes from Northville to Lake Placid," said Taylor's grandfather. "It's over one hundred miles. I've hiked quite a few portions of it."

No wonder he's in such good shape, I thought. The guy knows everything and goes everywhere.

"Anyway, when Kevin was about eight or nine, we did that hike into Tyrell Pond on a hot August day."

"Very buggy," I said.

"And very hot," said my mom. "We all brought our bathing suits because Tyrell Pond has a nice sandy bottom and it's encircled by these beautiful mountains."

"I've been there," said Taylor's grandfather. "It's gorgeous. One of the park's best swimming ponds."

"So, it kept getting hotter and hotter, and as we got closer to the pond, we heard voices and splashing."

"I couldn't wait to jump in," I said. "And I hate mountain ponds and lakes."

"My husband was the first one to get to the pond, and he immediately made the universal sign to be quiet."

"I thought there was a killer or a bear there or something," I said.

"Such a typical boy," laughed Taylor.

"But when I caught up to my husband, I could see there were two boys and two girls, college kids, just splashing around in the water with no clothes. They didn't know we were there, so we sort of quietly snuck away."

Everyone laughed.

We made a quick stop at Indian Lake to refill our water bottles and eat some cookies, granola bars, and orange slices. While coming back from one of the port-a-potties, I passed by my mom and Jacques standing alone and quietly talking.

"He must have noticed something," said my mom.

I couldn't believe what I was hearing, and although I wanted to stay and listen more, I quickly turned and walked away from them as quietly as possible in the opposite direction. Taylor was standing with her grandfather, and they were both eating a chocolate chip cookie. They nodded in my direction as I approached them. "Are you ready for that big downhill?" asked her grandfather.

"I hope so," I said.

When he walked away to get a bottle of Gatorade, I leaned in close to Taylor and said, "I just overheard the two of them talking. I'll bet he wants to go back to that pond with her."

"What?" Taylor looked at me with wide eyes.

"Tyrell Pond. Where I saw the skinny dippers."

"They're not going back to that pond," she said with a big smile on her face.

I took a sip from my water bottle. "Probably not," I said, "but I heard him mumble something."

"Well, that's gross."

We both just stood there quietly for a few seconds. "My dad isn't paying much attention to any of us right now, but he's a heck of a lot better than Jacques."

Taylor just nodded her head, and we both stood there in an awkward silence.

"How's your boyfriend doing?" I asked. It was something I had been thinking about lately, but was afraid to bring up. I guess thinking about Jacques got me thinking about Taylor's boyfriend, the soccer player.

"He's okay. He's at some soccer camp at Union College, and every night he calls to tell me about how great he played. He doesn't ask me much about where we are or how far we've biked."

"Typical guy," I said. "We're still just evolving, trying desperately to catch up to you women."

"That's right," laughed Taylor. "I bet you have a nice girlfriend."

"I'm between girlfriends right now," I said, amazed that I could so easily tell such a blatant lie.

"Sometimes it's nice to be single. I've been dating Drew for a year now. Some days I get tired of having to text or call him. Some days I just want to be left alone, but I like going to movies with him and it's nice to walk around Saratoga and go to a coffee shop. He has his own car."

"Yeah, I know what you mean," I said. "It's nice to have someone to hang out with, but during the track and cross-country season, I like being single so I can concentrate on running." I almost began laughing because stuff was coming out of my mouth that was absolutely insane.

Murray ambled over toward us looking like his dog had just died. "I have a flat tire," he said. "I don't know how to change a flat."

Taylor and I just sort of looked at him and shrugged. "I think my grandfather can change a flat."

"Murray, I can change your flat." It was my mom walking back with Jacques close beside her.

"You know how to change a flat?" I asked.

"I taught myself how to do it this spring in our garage. Don't you remember me telling you that? I offered to show you how, but you never seemed to care."

I vaguely remembered her saying something about changing a flat tire, but it was in the middle of track season and I had homework. Mainly I just wasn't interested.

"Where's your bike?"

Murray brought my mom over to his bike. The tire was completely flat and resting on its rim.

"Do you have a spare tube?"

Murray reached into his pack and brought out a spare tube, and for the next fifteen minutes, my mom went about changing that flat tire like she was performing brain surgery. We all just stood around and marveled at how accomplished she was. Even Taylor's grandfather praised her when he came upon us. "That's good work," he said.

"Here, Murray, take my air pump and fill the rest of the tire," said my mom, handing her pump over. "My hands are dirty, and I want to wash them."

As she walked away Jacques said, "Is there anything that woman can't do?" He said it loud enough for everyone around us to hear. Murray and Taylor even clapped for her. My mom gave a quick wave with the back of her hand and disappeared inside the ladies' room to get cleaned up. I wanted to get in Jacques' face and say, "Yeah, the one thing she can't do is marry you." But I just angrily chewed on a granola bar instead.

Back on the bikes. we pedaled toward the town of North Creek.

"When do we start with the big downhill?" asked Jacques.

"In about eight miles," said Murray.

"How is that tire riding?" asked my mom.

Murray looked down at the wheel. "As good as new. You're my hero."

The terrain seemed to go mostly down, so we all downshifted our bikes to get as much power as we could from each pedal. The road was in good shape, much better than most of the dilapidated houses we were passing, and I could tell we were picking up some good speed as we sailed down Route 28. This was our third day biking, and my legs felt pretty good, but the left side of my neck was still very stiff and sore.

"Let's give ourselves enough space as our speed picks up," shouted Taylor's grandfather. "I've got us at about twenty-two right now."

I thought of the TV images of those bikers in the Tour de France as they raced forty and fifty miles an hour down steep, curving mountains only a few inches apart. Here we were starting to go sixteen and seventeen, and now twenty miles an hour, and we seemed to be too close to each other.

"Now we're starting the big downhills," yelled Murray into the wind. He was riding in front of our group of six. None of us were talking. We held on to our bikes with all our strength, and I was so happy I didn't have an odometer and had no temptation to keep looking down to see how fast we were going. This section of the road was a bit cracked, and with the cars and trucks going by us, I was very tense. This felt like something my mother wouldn't want me to do, and I glanced to my left and there she was staring ahead with enormously wide-eyes.

The road was a pretty straight downhill, and I could see riders in groups of two, three, and four far ahead of us. All riding single file. I was concentrating mostly on the road and looking out for any big potholes or frost heaves. I was pedaling infrequently, but I could feel my speed picking up more and more. Murray was now in the lead, with Jacques about fifteen yards directly behind him. My mother was now about the same distance behind Jacques, and then there was a bigger gap, maybe ten or twenty yards, where Taylor, her grandfather, and I rode near each other in single file.

I heard the big truck behind me long before I ever saw it. From the sound of the engine, I knew it was one of those big sixteen-wheelers, and it was coming along very fast. I had already noticed on this ride how those big trucks create such a strong wind when they zoom past, that they can actually knock you off balance, and when I heard that thing coming up alongside me, I held on to my handlebars with all my strength. The swoosh from the truck was strong especially with my fast speed going down that hill. I could feel my bike wobbling a bit, but I kept it straight and took a deep, calming breath when the truck moved by me, Taylor's grandfather, and finally Taylor.

"Jesus, could you get any closer," yelled out Taylor's grandfather.

I kept following that big silver truck that looked as large as a NASA rocket. It was too close to the white line. My mom, Jacques and Murray weren't too far ahead, and that truck needed to move toward the center yellow line. It was much too close. It first passed by my mom, and she fought to keep her balance and stay upright, and then as the truck moved by Jacques, he seemed to hit some gravel on the side of the road and was completely out of control. His front wheel was all over the place. All I could think was that he was going to fall, and at this speed, that would be horrific. He tried to regain his balance and straighten out his front tire. "Don't brake!" I yelled into the wind, and then he disappeared off the road and down a grassy embankment.

CHAPTER 8

My mom screamed, and then Taylor screamed. We were all going so fast that it took us a while to slow our bikes down, and when I biked past the place where Jacques had crashed, I could see him sprawled out in tall grass at the bottom of a small hill. His twisted bike was to his left as he lay on his stomach like he had been hit by an assassin's bullet.

My mom was the first one off her bike. She dropped it to the ground and ran back to see if he was okay. I placed my bike next to hers and jogged back and then down the grassy hill to Jacques. He was stirring, letting out a deep groan, but he was holding his right shoulder and his left knee. When he rolled on his back, his knee had a long trail of blood coming down his shins and the back of his leg. My mom was the first one to get to him, and she cradled his head in her arms, asking over and over if he was okay.

Slowly Jacques sat up and moved his head in one big circle. He tried to take off his bike helmet, but his hands were shaking, his fingers unable to open the clasp. "Did anyone get a video of that?" he asked, moving his jaw around to see if it still worked. Murray, Taylor, and her grandfather had all arrived on the scene and were standing around looking down at him. "Because if there's a video, I don't want to ever watch it."

"Don't move," said my mom, who had now taken off her bike shirt to wipe the blood off his legs. She was now only wearing her black sports bra.

Jacques gave her a sort of wink and attempted to stand up.

"Not so fast," said Murray, who bent down to help him up. He even gave Jacques a kiss and sort of cuddled him. It caught me a bit off guard. I never thought Canadians were so affectionate.

Other bikers had now stopped on the road, and they were shouting down to see how he was doing. Jacques was standing now and waved at them. "I'm all right," he said, giving them a thumbs up. Murray was mostly holding him up.

"But your bike isn't," said Taylor's grandfather. The handlebars were bent, and so was his front tire. "You won't be able to ride this."

When I heard that, I must admit a part of me was happy because I figured Jacques would be done with this ride, and he'd go home to wherever he lived and we'd never hear from him again.

"I called the sag wagon," yelled one of the bikers from the road. "They'll be here in a few minutes."

The sag wagon was a truck that followed behind everyone and picked up bikers when they had an emergency or couldn't complete that day's ride.

"Maybe they can get my bike somewhere so it can be fixed," said Jacques with a grimace. He was now moving his tongue around his teeth to feel if they were all there.

"Maybe they can," said my mother, "but we have to get you checked out first. You'll need an x-ray, and maybe a few stitches in that knee."

"No, please no," said Jacques in a half-joking way. "I've heard about how bad your health care is in this country. No one will ever hear from me again."

"Very funny," said my mom. "Murray, you'll probably want to go along with him to make sure he doesn't end up in some doctor's waiting room for the rest of his life."

"But what about my bike?"

Murray took out his information sheet. "It says North Creek has a bike mechanic at the rest stop. Maybe he's a miracle worker who can get it fixed."

⬤

When the sag wagon arrived, Murray helped Jacques into the truck and told the driver to drop off the bike at the North Creek rest stop only a few miles away from where we were.

"He needs to get checked out by a doctor," said my mom.

"There's a clinic in Warrensburg," said the driver.

We all helped load Jacques's damaged bike and Murray's bike into the wagon. I gave him my plastic jacket to wear. "I'll let you know how everything's going," Murray said as he moved in next to Jacques.

Before they drove away, Jacques rolled down his window and said, "I appreciate all your help. I hope I haven't ruined your day." I could see his eyes sort of glistening, and for the first time I actually felt kind of sorry for him. Not much, I suppose, but I didn't want to see him hurt. Just gone.

"You didn't ruin our day," said Taylor's grandfather stressing the word "our".

"I'll take care of your bike," said my mom, and then the wagon moved down Route 28 on its way to North Creek. I didn't know if I should wave or not, but I did see Jacques hold his head and then sort of lean into Murray's arms as they pulled away. I must have been scrunching my face up a bit.

"What's the matter?" asked my mom. "I thought you knew that Murray and Jacques were partners."

The four of us were a bit slow as we got back on our bikes. "Did anyone get that license plate number?" asked my mom. "It was almost like that truck driver did it on purpose."

Taylor's grandfather nodded his head in agreement.

"I've had problems with drivers sharing the road. A lot of them think bikers should only be on bike paths."

For the next few miles, we biked in silence as we kept the rapids of the Hudson River on our left. I guess we were all thinking about how hurt Jacques might be, but also how lucky he was. I was also thinking how clueless I was about Jacques and Murray. It had never occured to me they were partners. I thought they were just friends.

The three of us stood around drinking and munching some granola bars. My mom and Mr. McCabe then walked over to the bike mechanic who was busy working on Jacques' damaged bike.

When they were gone Taylor walked over to me with a big smile. "I didn't know they were partners either."

I just shook my head. "So I guess my mom and Jacques."

"Yeah, it's nothing," said Taylor. "They've just become friends like you and me."

I scratched my head and smiled. I could also feel some of my worries kind of slip away.

"The mechanic thinks he can fix the bike, but it's going to take a few hours," said Mr. McCabe.

"Well, that's good," said Taylor.

"He'll bring it to the base camp in Warrensburg tonight." said my mom.

"Now let's hope the doctor can fix Jacques," said Taylor's grandfather.

The day warmed up nicely, enough for us to remove our jackets, and we left our bikes down by the train station to check out Main Street. There was a big hotel called the Copperfield almost directly across from the train station, and Mr. McCabe wanted to eat lunch there, but I reminded him there was a good café just down the street. I had never been to North Creek in the summer, and the place was hopping. The street seemed to be filled with those Adirondack general stores that sell everything from kayaks to pizza. There were also a few antique shops, and I know my mom normally would have been checking every one of them. This town also knew the bike ride was coming through today, and they had some guy sitting on the porch of a store playing old guitar favorites my mother would have loved. Most of the stores had sales, and there were these "Welcome Biker" signs all over the place. Main Street was crawling with people wearing tight-fitting spandex bike shorts, and the locals seemed to be having a fun time staring at how ridiculous we looked.

Café Sarah was crowded, but we were lucky to find an outdoor table to eat our sandwiches and drink our iced teas. My mom tried to make a call, but couldn't get through. She then tried to text his friend, but the Wi-Fi service was spotty at best. We had already biked about thirty miles, and we had eighteen or nineteen more, but I felt like this had been our longest day so far. I had just put my mouth around that delicious ham and cheese sub, when my mom's phone rang.

"Hi, how's it going?" She put Murray on speaker phone so everyone could hear.

"Jacques is gonna be okay." As she spoke, the service would sometimes die and then kick back in like a bad reception for a car radio. "He has a sprained shoulder and shouldn't be biking tomorrow. He also has five stitches by his left knee. He's sore and bruised, but nothing's broken inside or out."

Before I could say anything, Jacques yelled out in the background. "I'm biking tomorrow." That brought a smile to all our faces. Mr. McCabe was shaking his head.

"No, you heard the doctor," said Murray. " Anyway, we'll be at the doctor's for another hour or so. They're checking to see if he has a concussion, but I told them you need to have a brain to have a concussion. Any word on his bike?"

Mr. McCabe leaned in close to the phone. "The mechanic believes he can have it working for tomorrow."

"Well, he won't be using it tomorrow, but maybe for that last day," said Murray. "He's going to be very sore tomorrow while riding in the sag wagon."

"I'll be biking tomorrow," yelled Jacques. He seemed to be a good distance from the phone, and they sounded like an old bickering couple. "This doctor's office is very nice and only about a mile from the high school. We'll probably get a ride there when we're done. If you get there before me, just get my bag from the truck. I'll keep my phone handy if you need me."

Murray then said goodbye and signed off.

"Well, that Jacques is lucky to have someone like Murray in his life," said Taylor.

I quickly looked over at my mom and saw her nod her head.

When everyone was just about done eating, I excused myself and went to the men's room. After I shut and locked the door, I immediately texted my dad. *We had a bike rider friend who got hurt today. I think it shook mom up a bit. You should call her tonight and check in with her.*

I then noticed I had received an email from Dipper. *When are you finishing in the Strawberry Preserve?*

I actually laughed when I saw that, but texted back anyway. If I didn't, I was sure Dipper would look for a place called the Strawberry Preserve. *Not Strawberry! It's the Corning Preserve in Albany, and I'll be there some time on Thursday, maybe around noon.*

Mr. McCabe talked to the mechanic one more time about Jacques' bike, and then we reluctantly got back on our bikes for the nineteen-mile ride to Warrensburg. This was our third straight day of biking, and my legs, my butt, my neck, and my wrists were starting to throb again, making nineteen miles seem like a long way to pedal. There also seemed to be very little flat. It was either uphill or downhill, and because it was later than usual, it was getting sunny and warm. The four of us were mostly quiet as we continued our journey through Weavertown, then to The Glen with the Hudson River now on our right. We weren't passing many bikers on this leg of the trip, but a few passed us and periodically yelled "On your left." We'd move over only to see a biker that didn't look very fit at all zoom by us.

We were now going up a long, steady hill where Route 28 merges into Route 9 when Taylor let out a complaining groan. "Will this ride never end?"

As we approached the somewhat bustling town of Warrensburg, we realized we hadn't seen so many people or cars since the day we left Lake Placid. "I never thought Warrensburg was a big city till now," I said.

"Yeah," said Taylor. "I already miss the quiet of the Adirondacks."

"We're still in the Adirondacks," said her grandfather.

Warrensburg didn't have the calm of North Creek or Blue Mountain Lake. Route 9 was a bit of a traffic jam with tourists pouring in for the summer. It seemed noisy and confusing, probably my perception had changed because we had spent a few days in quiet towns on quiet roads. Cars were pulling into the McDonald's on our left and the Price Chopper on our right. They were cutting in front of us and drivers were giving us nasty looks. I was so happy to finally make it to the Warrensburg High School on Schroon River Road. We pulled our bikes around to the back of the school to find we wouldn't get our usual choice of select spots. It was already crowded with numerous tents, and there was even a long line at the truck showers, but at least it was much quieter than Route 9.

"We have to bike on that road tomorrow to reach Lake George," grumbled my mom.

"It'll be early in the morning. Won't be so bad," said Taylor's grandfather.

"Some of those trucks had such wide mirrors. I thought I was gonna get hit," I said.

"We take a chance every day we get out of bed," replied Taylor's grandfather, and I thought of how tough this old, gray-haired guy was. Here was someone who was a widower, and if that's not bad enough, his daughter and her husband die in a car crash, forcing him, late in life, to raise another child. His great-great grandparents were enslaved, owned by other people, and he even defended the country he lived in and was actually in the military to defend it. And the only time he complained on this trip was about Jacques, and who could blame him there? He never complained about the heat, or the hills, or the chilly mornings. He must have been around seventy years old, but still put up his own tent every afternoon and took it down every morning, and ate whatever was put in front of him.

We leaned our four bikes against a few trees in the back and went to get our bags from the truck. Murray and Jacques were nowhere in sight, and it took a few trips to get all the bags we needed. I put my tent up first, and attempted to put up my mom's tent since she was still in the shower truck. It was driving me crazy and I was ready to throw it in the stream behind me, but Taylor came over to help, and instead of getting frustrated, we laughed at how much of a struggle we were having. I loved it when she laughed. Her eyes just sort of lit up, and the whole world around her seemed to be such a better place. When Mr. McCabe finished putting up his tent, he also came over to help.

"Now, Kevin, I thought you knew what you were doing, but I can see that you're completely lost."

I was laughing hysterically. "Completely lost, but I had you fooled."

Even Taylor threw up her hands. "How does your mom do this every morning?"

"I don't know," I said. "She can even change a bike tire."

It took another twenty minutes, but the three of us finally got my mom's tent up. We threw her clothes bag in there, which sealed our victory like a three-point shot at the buzzer, and then Taylor and I walked over to the shower truck to clean up. The girls line was on the right; the boys line to the left. There were a few people ahead of us. We each gave a sort of wave as we entered almost simultaneously inside the truck. My third day in the shower truck, and I really didn't care anymore who was in there and what they saw because the warm water felt so soothing on my sore muscles. I just stood under the water and let it go down over the top of my head. I could have stayed there for days, and began to feel sad because there were only two more nights before the trip would finish in Albany. And what would happen then? Would my parents stay together? Would this bike trip be the final straw to whatever kept them together? Would I ever hear from Taylor again? Would it be awkward to see her at a cross-country meet? Would we be good friends for the rest of our lives or only a distant memory? Would Jacques become part of my life in some way, or would he disappear like a mole back into Ottawa? If I stayed in that shower truck and never came out, then I'd never have to face any of those problems, but instead I turned off the water and walked out of the shower stall to dry up and get back to living my life.

Murray and Jacques showed up an hour later. The four of us were sitting on a bench near our tents when we saw a car slowly drive up and let the two of them out. Murray's bike sat securely in a rack in the back of the car. We all waved and yelled out their names.

Murray called over to us as he took his bike off the rack, and Jacques forced a wave despite having his right shoulder bandaged and his arm in a sling. His left knee had a large white bandage over it with a slight trace of red peeking through. They slowly walked over to us, or in Jacques's case, hobbled, and we all stood up like a judge had entered a courtroom.

Murray reached for his phone and took a picture. "I can't wait to post this!"

"You better say I was run over by a truck," said Jacques, trying to force a smile. I could tell that every step hurt, but he kept walking anyway.

"Sit down." My mom held him by the arm and placed him on the bench. "Murray, do you have any power over this stubborn man?"

Murray shook his head. "Not much."

My mom sat down next to him. "He's still talking about biking the next two days."

"The doctor says I can do it if I go slow and take my time. See I can even bend my knee." He slowly bent his knee and he also made a pretty obvious grimace.

"If you fall again there's no telling what might happen to you."

Jacques sat there looking straight ahead, his eyes watery. "I don't want to get too emotional," he began, attempting to control himself, "but finishing this trip is very important to me. I've had a history of not finishing a lot of things. Murray knows what I'm talking about. So I'm going to ride tomorrow and the next day, and if I have to ride alone while you go on ahead, so be it. It might take me all day, but I'm going to make it to Albany."

The four of us just stood there trying not to stare at both of them on the bench. "I'll ride with him," said Murray.

"I'll ride with him," said Taylor's grandfather.

"I'll ride with him," said Taylor.

"So will I." I was only going to do it because of Taylor. I glanced at my mom, who glared at me.

She just shook her head. "This is ridiculous. We're encouraging this fool to hurt himself even more."

And that's when Jacques stood up and said, "I am Spartacus!"

A few other bikers near us heard this bandaged man, and a few of them yelled out, "No, I am Spartacus!"

And soon we were all laughing and yelling out that we were Spartacus. When the laughter subsided, Jacques sat back down and said, "I'll start the ride tomorrow and see how it goes. If I'm too sore or can't do it, then the sag wagon can pick me up. You don't have to ride with me."

"I'm ready for an easy day," said Murray.

"And there's a great brew pub in Glens Falls just off from the bike trail," said Taylor's grandfather.

"A brew pub, huh?" said Jacques. "Well, I'll at least make it to the brew pub. After an hour or two there, the sag wagon may need to pick me up."

We laughed again.

We spent a quiet afternoon by the tent. Murray offered to help Jacques in the shower, but Jacques declined. Jacques was moving slowly, but he was moving. Just before dinner the bike mechanic drove up with Jacques' bike on his rack. "I had all the parts I needed," he said. "It just took some time to get it done." He handed Murray the bike and Jacques the receipt for the work.

Jacques looked longingly at his bike with the new handlebars and the new chain and front tire. "You even cleaned it!" He shook hands with the mechanic. "Well, now I've got to ride. There's no excuse."

We had a turkey and beef dinner at the school cafeteria, and after dinner, a professor from Plattsburgh spoke on the importance of Lake George in both the French and Indian and the Revolutionary wars. He showed slides on the big screen in the auditorium. I knew that Lake George was an important historical place, but I never realized how important it had been. I always thought of it as a fun place my parents and I used to visit every summer to go swimming and then walk around the tacky T-shirt shops while we ate our ice cream cones. Sure, a replica of Fort William Henry stood high on a grassy hill overlooking the lake, and as a kid I loved to hear the cannons go off, but I never understood its importance in American history until now.

On Your Left

The professor had that intellectual look like 'I'm so smart, I don't have to comb my hair anymore,' and he loved to say big words like "malcontent" and "nefarious." He went on and on about how the lake had once been a popular hunting ground for the Iroquois and the Algonquin Indians, and that Father Isaac Jogues was the first white man to see the lake in 1646.

"He was a Frenchman," whispered Jacques to all of us as he gave a thumbs-up sign.

The professor mentioned that Father Jogues named the lake Lac du Sacrement, which is what it was called till 1755, when Sir William Johnson named it Lake George in honor of Britain's King George ll.

"Now the Brits had it," whispered Murray, flashing his thumb to all of us.

The professor went on to explain, in rather graphic detail, some of the major Revolutionary War battles in 1755 and 1780. He mentioned that we'd be biking the next day right by the area where British Colonel Ephraim Williams was killed, and it all began to sound so depressing—we've been killing each other for hundreds of years. I wondered what those soldiers must have thought back in the middle to late 1700's when they saw how beautiful that lake was without all those tacky shirt and souvenir stores. They probably couldn't even see the beauty because they were so afraid of getting killed. What would they think today if they saw the big passenger steamboats and the people laying on the beach in their skimpy bathing suits or waterskiing and parasailing up and down the lake? I bet they'd be pretty depressed to have been born at that time and not today.

The professor talked about the importance of Lake George and nearby Lake Champlain, and how it was all part of gaining control of the Hudson River. Apparently, if you controlled the water, you controlled what went up or downstream, and this gave your army amazing power. He also talked about the book *The Last of the Mohicans* by James Fennimore Cooper and something called the Bloody Pond, where over two hundred French soldiers were killed. I was starting to think how haunted that lake and those places around it must be.

When I got back to my tent, it was after 9:00 p.m. and starting to get dark The almost full moon was slowly rising in the east, and I was tired. Taylor was on the phone, probably with soccer boy. Murray was giving Motrin to Jacques, who was complaining about taking them. My mom was quietly talking to my father, and Taylor's grandfather sat outside his tent with a flashlight reading a history book written by the Plattsburgh professor, who, after his talk, hung around a while and sold and signed copies of it. It had only been three days, but I felt like the six of us had become some type of disjointed family that, in a strange way, had grown to care about each other. And it was nice to feel like I was in a family again. I hadn't felt that way in a few years.

I posted a picture of tent city with some mountains in the background and wrote, *"We made it to Warrensburg. Tomorrow, 45 miles, we ride through Lake George and finish at the Saratoga Battlefield."*

Dipper had written back earlier in the evening. *"Dwight was running at the town park and turned his ankle this morning. It was bad. I told him that you were going to be our top runner now, and he said, 'There's no way I'll ever let Kevin Walsh beat me in a cross country race.' He was also laughing about you doing a bike trip with your mom. I told him I thought it was pretty cool and that you were biking a lot of miles. He laughed at that too and tried to get some of the other guys to laugh with him. He really can be a prick at times. Just thought you might want to know. How does your butt feel after all the biking?"*

I just sat back in my tent and thought how wonderful it would be to run past Dwight Woodard in a race. He was one of the top runners in our area and even our state. He would probably get a scholarship to a Division 1 college, and he would be so shocked to see my long, uncoordinated legs move past him. I'd love to see his expression. And Dipper was right, Dwight was pretty much a prick. He rarely ever said more than a few words to me, and now he was making fun of me because of this bike trip. That's typical of him. He's always making fun of someone.

I wrote back to the Dipper. *"Sorry to hear about*

Dwight. We need him to be healthy if we have any chance to win sectionals. How's your running going? My butt is pretty sore, but only two more days. I can finish!"

I checked Facebook before putting my phone away. My Aunt Agnes gave me a like. For someone in her eighties, she was pretty hip for checking things online. I read a few things on Instagram, looked through some pictures I had taken on my phone, and after about thirty minutes, I turned off my flashlight and yelled goodnight to my mom in the tent next to me. I heard a weak "Goodnight," echo back in return. I lay there in the dark, a few random coughs, some low talk in the tents near me, and a few random tent zippers going up or down, but it was mostly quiet. In the far distance cars continued going north and south on the Northway, which reminded me that tomorrow we would be heading into one of the most crowded areas of our trip. We'd be leaving this wonderful Adirondack Park with its six million acres, and even though I tried to think good thoughts as I lay there, all I could think about were bloody ponds and soldiers being ambushed and screams and death in this cathedral of natural beauty with all those thousands upon thousands of tall evergreen trees. And I pictured Jacques going down that embankment, now bloodied and bandaged like an old French soldier, and hoped no one would get hurt tomorrow.

CHAPTER 9

DAY 4: WARRENSBURG TO
SARATOGA BATTLEFIELD (45 MILES)

"How are you feeling?" my mom said just above a whisper the next morning. There was barely any light out yet.

"Like I fell off a bike and landed in a ditch going thirty miles an hour," answered Jacques in a somewhat less muffled tone.

"I'll walk over to the bathroom with you," my mom said. All I could hear was a sort of groan from Jacques, and then it was completely quiet.

I reached for my cell phone to see what time it was and noticed that my dad sent me a text after I fell asleep. *Kevin, have a great ride today. Think of me when you bike through Lake George. That's where I first took you miniature golfing. I can't wait to hear all about your trip. Not going has been one of the biggest mistakes I've ever made. I love you—Dad.*

I read that message three times. My eyes actually teared up a bit. *Dad, I remember that day we played golf. I've also missed you this week, and these last few years. We're doing ok. Today it's 45 miles and not too hilly. Should be an easier day. Kevin*

I looked at that message and then erased it and wrote another one.

Dad, thanks for the nice email. I still remember that day we played miniature golf. We're doing ok. I love you too!

And I sent it.

When I was taking down my tent, Taylor popped her head out of hers like a bird coming out of a birdhouse. Her long hair was kind of scrunched up and her eyes were still sleepy looking—and I honestly don't think I've ever seen anything as beautiful as that.

"Morning," I said.

She crawled out and smiled at me. She wore these cute, pink running shorts and a Freihofer's Run for Women shirt. "Right back at you."

"It's going to be nice to sleep in your own bed again, isn't it?" I was taking the rain fly off the top of my tent.

She did some slow yoga stretches for her back and legs. "I'm gonna miss the sound of the night. I love to wake up at night in a tent and hear all the noises and things moving around in the woods." She said this with only one eye open.

It's strange, but I was actually enjoying the sleep-walking way of taking down my tent every morning and setting it up every afternoon. I can see how people who backpack across Europe can actually have fun. Murray had now come out of his tent and was clearing his throat. He nodded at the two of us. "Where's the bandaged bandito?"

I looked at the school just as Jacques and my mom slowly walked in our direction. "Here he comes now."

"How goes it?" asked Murray.

Jacques no longer wore the arm sling. "If you get me more of that Motrin, I think I'll be just fine."

"He's having a hard time walking," said my mom.

"But I won't be walking today, I'll be biking. And with help." Jacques held out his hand as Murray placed four Motrin in his palm.

Taylor's grandfather now came out of the tent he shared with Taylor. He looked the same in the morning as he did at night. "There's no shame in resting up and taking a ride in the wagon today."

Jacques placed two Motrin in his mouth and was about to drink from his water bottle. "Come on, James. Are you gonna tell me you'd ever do that? If you were me, you'd be riding today, too. Or at least trying."

Taylor's grandfather just sort of shrugged, and we all knew that it would have to be a very serious injury to keep him from a ride.

It took Jacques a long time to get dressed for the day, and quite a few guttural groans escaped his tent.

"How's it going?" said Murray into the tent flap. "Great."

"Do you need help?"

"I can manage," said Jacques with another groan.

My mother was not enjoying any of this. "Jacques, this is ridiculous! I can't believe we're condoning this by offering to help you."

"You don't have to help me." When he emerged from the tent, he looked fairly respectable, except for the bandaged knee and scrapes on both elbows. His shoulder was still taped up, but it was mostly under his bike shirt.

At breakfast, it was like sitting with royalty. Many bikers, who heard about the crash, visited Jacques. Even Mr. Jacobs, my friend from Virginia, stopped by to see how Jacques was doing. The bikers asked all sorts of questions. "What can I do for you?" "How are you doing today?" "How is your bike?" "That trucker should be fined for driving that close to bikers!" "We need to have more bike trails and bike lanes in this country!"

Jacques just sat there answering all their questions and enjoying the attention. People waited on him, getting him orange juice and coffee and asking if he needed another bagel. My mother sat there shaking her head and saying to me, "Don't grow up to be one of those typical, stubborn men."

I smiled, but inside, I worried that I had already become one.

Mr. No Personality Al went over the day's agenda with that lousy microphone of his. He explained, in detail, the 45-mile ride, finishing up with a quick talk about the elevation gains and losses. Today would be mostly downhill, although at the end we would be climbing from the little town of Fort Edward to the Saratoga Battlefield.

"You Americans love to make national parks out of your battlefields, don't you?" said Jacques.

"You do the same thing in Canada," said Taylor's grandfather.

"Yeah, but we don't have as many battlefields."

We all helped take down Jacques' tent and put it away in the bag and then it was time to begin our ride. We were starting a bit later than normal due to Jacques' injury, making it feel warmer as we stood with our bikes about to begin our fourth day of touring.

"You don't have to do this," said my mom one last time.

"Yes, I do," said Jacques, and with that, he straddled his legs over the bike frame. "It feels pretty good." He was trying to be extra cheery, but his face was all scrunched up in some real agony, and then after a few unsteady wobbles he took off back down Schroon River Road in the direction of Route 9 and Lake George Village.

Surprisingly, we began at a pretty good clip, and the first five miles was all downhill to the village of Lake George. Jacques rode in the front, where we could keep an eye on him, while we were spread out behind him. I was third in line, and could easily tell that Jacques tried not to grip his handlebars with all his strength. We were probably going sixteen or seventeen miles an hour down the hill, and when we came in to the village, there were actually people on the sides of the road clapping for us. It sent a chill up my spine, the same way I often felt as I finished a big cross-country race or a crowded road race. Jacques even waved to the crowd and yelled out a few bonjours.

After a quick ride through the village, we followed the signs and turned left toward the public beach. The six of us stopped right in front of the re-built Fort William Henry, which had the numbers 1755 imprinted on the raised grass in front of it. Behind it, Lake George spread north for thirty-two miles. It was scattered throughout with a dozen or so small islands. I never really took the time to notice how pretty this lake actually is, and for the first time I could see why it's called the Queen of America's Lakes. The big ships waited in port to fill up their decks for a cruise around the lake. Every now and then, their horns let loose an exploding boom that echoed across town.

"I never get tired of how beautiful this place is, even with all those corny stores and fast-food places," said my mom.

"But can you imagine how beautiful it would be if the French had won that war and this was in our control," said Jacques. "We would have left the nature alone."

"Well, I guess we'll never know," said Taylor's grandfather.

Other bikers also stopped to look at the blue choppy water that seemed to go on forever. "I went snorkeling in this lake last year," said one biker. "You can get down to the bottom and see some of the remains of those old wooden boats. They call them bateaux. It's amazing."

"Can you imagine what it must have looked like to see hundreds of those war ships sailing up to Lake Champlain?" said another.

The sun was warm on my shoulders, and the sky was blue. I would have enjoyed biking a half-mile down to the Million Dollar Beach to swim for a few hours. I would love to just spend the day with Taylor. And before I knew what I was doing, I said, "What time does that beach open?"

Murray whipped out his agenda sheet from inside the waist of his bike shorts. "Let's see. Today, it opens at 9:00 am for any bikers who want to swim, but 10:00 a.m. for the public."

"That's in fifteen minutes," I said. "Taylor, what if the two of us hang out here and swim for a few hours?" I can't believe I actually said such a thing. A few days ago, I would never have been able to say anything like that.

My mom looked at me. "I only have five dollars to give you."

Murray continued reading from the agenda. "The beach is free for the bikers."

"I don't have a swimsuit. It's on the bus," said Taylor.

"We can swim in our bike shorts."

"I don't like the two of you biking alone," said Taylor's grandfather. "Route 4 is narrow, and there's not much of a shoulder."

"Hey, I'm stopping for a beer at the brew pub," said Jacques, "and if you're biking with me today, then you're going very slow. They'll probably catch us before we ever get to the battlefield."

"We'll only stay for a few hours," I said. I could feel myself getting more and more excited about spending time on this beach with just Taylor. "And you know there'll be other bikers around us when we start biking. They're finishing all day long."

"It would be kind of fun," Taylor said, looking directly at her grandfather.

"These two have been good sports the last few days hanging around with all the old people," said Jacques. "Let them go and have some fun."

"One hour," said her grandfather. "At 10:00, I want the two of you back on your bikes. I don't like that Route 4." He said this with the demeanor of a general giving instructions to his troops. And neither of us could disobey him.

"Yes, sir," I said with everything but the salute.

"One hour," said Taylor, who looked at me with a big smile.

"I only have a five-dollar bill," said my mom. "I

don't want to give you my debit card. I was going to take more money out at an ATM later today."

"Here's a twenty," said Taylor's grandfather. His eyes were bearing down on me. "I'll check in with you after thirty minutes to see how you're doing." And then he said directly to me. "Take good care of her. She's the most important thing in the world to me." He then walked over and gave Taylor the money and quietly to me he said, "I get nervous with Taylor in the north country here. I've seen more Confederate flags than I'd ever like to see. Keep your eyes out for any trouble."

That was a pretty intimidating thing to hear. "I will," I said.

"He will," said my mom, who must have overheard some of what was said.

Taylor and I waved goodbye, and as we pedaled to the public beach, I heard Jacques say, "We're still going to that brew pub."

"But it's too early for a beer," said my mom, and that was the last I could make out.

"What a great idea," said Taylor. We biked the short distance to the beach side since it was only nine in the morning and not many people were up and about in this crowded little Lake George Village.

"This is our last full day together, and I wanted to do something a little different." It felt kind of strange to be all alone with her after the crazy day we had just spent.

"Let's pretend we're boyfriend and girlfriend today," said Taylor.

My heart started drumming away in my chest. "Let's do that." I suppose a pretend girlfriend for a day was better than no real girlfriend ever.

We locked up our bikes on the bike rack out front and walked inside the beach's main building. There was a young guy, a few years older than me, at the desk wearing a green official-looking shirt that said *New York State Parks* on it. He was reading something on his cell phone, and when he looked up and noticed us he said, "Are you with the bike ride?"

"Yes," said Taylor. "I'm biking with my boyfriend." And she placed her right hand on my left shoulder.

If I could have had a video of her saying that, it would be something I'd watch every day for the rest of my life.

"Well, you're the first to get here today. It's free for you, and we'll even let you borrow some towels."

"Thanks," I said.

Before giving us the towels, he wanted to know how the ride had been going. We explained where we started and how far we had ridden already, and where we were ending up that day.

"Really," he said, "the Saratoga Battlefield?" As he said this, I noticed that he was checking out how pretty Taylor was. When he handed us the four towels, two for laying on and two for drying off, he showed us to the door that led to the men's and women's locker rooms. "Just follow the signs to the beach," he said. I thanked him for the towels and entered the men's locker room. It was empty, and I took a few minutes to go to the bathroom and wash my hands. I gave myself a big smile in the mirror and thought I was actually looking pretty good.

Taylor was waiting for me as I came out the locker room door. She had a big grin on her face. "We're the only people here."

"It's like having our own Caribbean island."

Two lifeguards walked by wearing orange bathing suits and hoodie pullovers. They nodded in our direction. "I'm glad to see our servants are here," said Taylor as quietly as possible, though I laughed out loud.

"Where would you like to place our towels, darling?"

Taylor scanned the completely empty beach. "Where to go? Where to go? Follow me, luv." And she walked down the stairs to some nice soft sand, where she spread out her towel. I spread my towel right next to hers. She had already removed her bike shoes and socks, and I sat down and did the same. She plopped down next to me on her towel and proceeded to whip off her shirt and sit there in her red sports bra. "It's kind of like a bathing suit top," she said, and all I could do was nod.

When I had finally pulled off my shoes and socks, Taylor said, "It's gonna be cold this early, but I think we should take a dip now and then lay around in the sun to dry off. I don't want to bike that far in wet shorts."

I thought that would be a great idea.

"Who invited those people to our private island?" said Taylor. She pointed to three other bikers, all men, who had also decided to swim for a while on today's bike ride. They nodded in our direction and we waved back.

For me, the worst part of going to the beach was removing my shirt. As a runner, I had strong legs, but my scrawny, white-as-vanilla-ice-cream chest embarrassed me. I'd usually take my shirt off and then jump in the water as quickly as possible. When I got out I'd dry up and put my shirt back on as fast as I could.

"Surf's up!" I screamed, as I tore off my shirt and ran into the water, diving out as far as I could and hopefully hiding my white scrawny chest.

I've been to this beach before with my family, always on hot, crowded days. The sand is usually blazing hot, and I would often hop from one foot to the other until I got to the water. This early in the morning, though, it was only about seventy degrees. The sand felt smooth and even a bit cool, and I had no fear running out into the water knowing the bottom here was also sandy. No errant logs or leeches. When I emerged from under the water, I moved around and floated a bit on my back, and that's when I heard a big splash in front of me. Taylor sped toward me like a cannonball from Fort William Henry. When she got to me, she erupted out of the water and placed her arms around my back and shoulders. Our legs were sort of entangled, and we looked directly into each other's eyes only a few inches apart. I could feel our body heat shoot through every fiber of my being. We just clung to each other like that for one, two, maybe five seconds, and then she opened her arms and moved away from me, floating back toward the beach. I had never before looked so deeply into the eyes of someone, and I could feel this powerful electric current going through us. I think Taylor felt it, too. Maybe that's why she pulled away.

"The water feels good," I said, once again floating on my back in water maybe five or six feet deep. A definite awkwardness had sprung up between us, and I wanted to get back to that playful mood of pretending to be a couple.

Taylor swam toward me and stopped a few feet away. "I can't be your girlfriend."

I tried to smile. "We're only pretending." I stopped floating and stood in front of her, never quite realizing how much taller I was.

"No, I mean in real life. I'd like to be your girlfriend, but I can't. We're at different schools. We're both going to college next year."

My heart was doing a different kind of banging in my chest now. It struck slower and sadder. Of course she couldn't be my girlfriend. Why would someone as beautiful as Taylor Lewis ever be interested in someone as dorky and ugly as me? I just stood there in that water, which felt much colder now and wished I could be beamed far away to never be seen again. Why couldn't Doctor Who show up and take me far away to a different time? If I had my running shoes, I'd put them on and run away, maybe up north to Canada where it's usually cold.

"Didn't you feel that?" asked Taylor, taking my hands in hers.

"I felt it—and it was the best feeling in the world."

"But I have a boyfriend, and we don't live that close to each other, and you probably don't even have a car. It will never work."

She might have kept talking indefinitely, justifying her reluctance, but I went for it. I took my hands from hers and enclosed them around her small, athletic back and shoulders. I didn't kiss her. I didn't know how to kiss a girl, not for real anyway, but I did give her as warm and loving a hug as I knew how, and she leaned in to my chest. We stood there for a few seconds and rocked back and forth in the water, and it seemed like time had stopped.

When we got back on the beach and dried off in a sun growing warmer with each minute I said, "I don't want this to be a weird day between us. I want us to have fun. We have a lot of biking to do, and if this is our last day together, then I want it to be a good one, because I feel so lucky to be spending the day with someone as as nice and as beautiful as you."

Taylor teared up, and I wiped away her tears with my white towel. We both sat down and looked out at the small waves rippling across Lake George. A few boats motored around on the blue water, and three boats pulled parasailers high above the water.

"I want this to be a perfect day, too." Taylor puckered her lips and smiled at me. "Do you really think I'm beautiful?"

"More beautiful than Lake George." After I said that, I pulled my shirt over my head, but before I could finish, Taylor interrupted me.

"Don't put your shirt on," she said. "I have some suntan lotion. I know. I'm black and I have suntan lotion. Kind of funny?"

"I hate being seen with my shirt off."

Taylor shook her head. "Don't say that. You look great with your shirt off."

"I'm all white and skinny. I bet your boyfriend doesn't look like this."

Taylor reached for her suntan lotion and laughed, "Well, he doesn't have white skin, and another difference is that my boyfriend would never say anything as nice as what you just said about me."

I took my shirt off and spread the lotion on my snow-white chest and shoulders.

We lay down on our backs, our arms shielding our eyes against the bright sun. Occasionally we'd talk and take a few pictures with our phones. I took a nice selfie of the two of us leaning together on our beach towels, but mostly we just lay there in the quiet listening to the water and birds overhead and the boats on the water, and I knew I would remember this day forever.

Around 10:30, and after Taylor had already received two calls from her grandfather, she sat up and said, "The food stand just opened. I'll buy you an ice cream."

I was a bit sleepy, and it was kind of hard to get back on my feet, but I joined her for an ice cream, and on our way walking there she reached out and took my hand in hers. I felt so proud—and that electricity between us hadn't diminished a bit. I didn't even worry about being late to leave for the Saratoga Battlefield. With Taylor, time just flew by.

My bike shorts were still a bit wet when we began the ride. It was a little after 11:00 and getting downright warm. As we pedaled along the shaded Warren County Bikeway, we got into a good groove and began knocking off mile after mile. It was nice to be on a bike trail with no car exhaust choking us. The paved trail was in excellent condition. For the first five or six miles, we didn't see many bikers from our group, but soon we came upon small groups of two or three.

They were mostly older or out of shape, and we zoomed past them like they were in slow motion. On the bike trail, we were able to bike next to each other, and it felt great to talk and bike fast at the same time. We talked about school and how much we had hated being online during Covid. Taylor described her friends. I told her about Doctor Who. She had never heard of it, and we laughed and got out of breath and our legs and our hearts were pumping, and we both said it felt like we were running a hard track workout at school.

We went from the Warren County Bikeway to Glens Falls, then to the Feeder Canal Heritage Trail, and finally, to the Old Champlain Canal Towpath. Just as we got on Route 4, there was a rest stop, but we were so late they were actually packing up a lot of it. We must have been one of the last fifty or sixty bikers to come through that day. The only stuff they had left was Gatorade, some granola bars, chocolate chip cookies, and watermelon slices. I was sick of all of it and the thought of eating one more granola bar was making me want to hurl.

It was now around noon, and I was getting very hungry for some real food. "Let's find a place to eat on Route 4."

We pooled our money, and had almost seventeen dollars left. "I'd love to find a pizza joint," said Taylor. "When I'm training hard, there's nothing like a good slice of pizza."

"Well, how about five or six slices of pizza?" I said and laughed.

Route 4 didn't have a very good shoulder to bike on, but there were a lot of old buildings and historical signs near the tiny but ancient-looking town of Fort

Edward. There were some great, Victorian-era homes with those wrap-around porches, the kind you want to put a rocking chair on and sit all day drinking cold glasses of lemonade. But right in the center of town, we were happy to come upon a small pizza place.

As we waited for our food, Taylor took out her cell phone and gave me a history lesson on Fort Edward. "This was the place where they would have to carry boats around the falls in the Hudson River. During the French and Indian War in 1755, a General Lyman built a fort here and called it Fort Lyman."

"He must have had a big ego," I said as I drank from my cold bottle of Coke.

"The next year it was renamed Fort Edward in honor of Prince Edward, the son of King George."

She kept reading out other pertinent historical facts, and I reached out my right hand to touch hers. "I love that you're interested in learning things. I love how smart you are." At that moment I loved every single thing about her, though I couldn't tell her that just yet.

Taylor looked up and put her phone away. "If I ever get married, I want to marry someone who wants to travel and do exciting things and learn about everything. That's what my parents were like."

"I want to marry someone who likes to run, enjoys going on biking trips and wants to travel and do exciting things and wants to learn about everything."

She threw her paper napkin at me. "You wouldn't want to marry me."

"Oh? Why?"

"Because I have a bad temper, and I always want my way, and anyway, I'm seventeen and not getting married till I'm in my thirties, and I might not even get married then. I also don't want to have any kids. I want to keep running and being athletic, and I don't think I have the patience for kids."

"I'd take care of our kids."

She just looked at me and gave a sort of half-smile.

The pizza came and just as we were about to eat, I received a text from my mom. "*It's been a slow day. We're outside Fort Edward. We spent an hour at the brewery. Jacques is in a lot of pain. We're averaging 10-12 miles an hour with many stops. Where are you?*"

I sent her a text about our day, but I never said we were also in Fort Edward. After we ate, Taylor called and spoke once again with her grandfather for a few minutes.

"I think we can catch them before they get to the battlefield," she said.

"So now the race is on," I laughed. The truth was that I really didn't want to catch them.

Taylor began counting out some money to pay our tab, and she stopped and looked at me. "The girl who marries you is going to be very lucky."

"Why?"

"Because you're kind, and you're sweet, and you notice things. You also don't have a big ego like most guys."

I shrugged, but what worried me was that my mom had said something similar to this about Jacques.

"You listen," said Taylor. "Most guys just want to talk. I can see you married and living in a nice suburban neighborhood with two kids, a boy and a girl, and you'll go to work every day and run at lunch, and you and your wife will have a date every Saturday night."

"That sounds pretty boring." I didn't know if I should be angry or not.

"And you'll be a great dad and your kids will love you, and your wife will look out the kitchen window and see the three of you building a snowman in the back yard, and she'll realize how lucky she is to have married someone as good as you."

"I'm not good at building snowmen. Their heads always fall off."

"And that will make her love you even more."

Without Murray, we had no idea how much more we had to bike. Neither of us had an odometer, so we had no idea how far we had already biked. We just kept plugging on, following the yellow circle markers in the road. Occasionally, we'd come upon some groups of bikers, and say hello, and wish them luck. We had to bike in single file because of the narrow shoulder, and I loved watching Taylor as she pedaled ahead of me. Her legs were strong, and I could have watched them move all day.

We biked by a series of canal locks on our right. The sun was really baking us on the road that had very little shade. It was pretty country, though, with the Vermont Green Mountains to our left and that sparkling water to our right.

When we finally left Route 4 and turned right on Route 69, we undertook a long uphill toward Route 32 and the Saratoga National Battlefield Road. We biked through a tiny town named Victory. It was mostly farmland on either side of us, but the road kept climbing, probably the most difficult biking we had done on the entire trip. Our speed was very slow. We weren't sitting much on this climb—mostly standing and pushing down those bike pedals with all the strength we had—and we were both sweating so much our hands were slipping on the handlebars. A scattering of bikers traveled far ahead of us, and because of these wet bike shorts, my butt was beginning to feel quite sore and chaffed up.

"I think I see them." Taylor nodded her head, and I looked a long way ahead to see four bikers moving very slowly. Sometimes we'd lose sight of them behind a tree or on a turn, but then they would reappear again. They were all bunched up, and it sure did look like our group.

"Let's catch them," I said, and Taylor immediately pedaled faster with me close behind. How could she have so much strength? It was like we were both in the lead of a cross country race and the finish line was just ahead of us and we were going as fast as possible, pushing each other to the limit to see who would break first and fall off the pace.

There weren't too many cars going by us now on this somewhat deserted road. "Did you see that?" Taylor's voice sounded a bit frightened.

"What?"

"That car that just went by us."

"It was silver."

"And it had a Confederate flag sticker on its bumper."

"Did it?" I said. I rarely notice things like that.

"It did," said Taylor, "and it's turning around and coming back at us."

She was right. The car had turned around and was coming back in our direction even slowing down a bit. It looked liked three, maybe four teenage boys in the car and the windows were down and two boys in the backseat were sticking their heads out.

"Whatever they say," said Taylor, "just keep biking. We're not too far from that group ahead of us and I think the battlefield is close by."

What was I going to say? I've lived most of my life avoiding any confrontation that came my way, and there were four of them in the car. It slowed down and one of the boys in the backseat yelled out, "Hey, Beyonce, where you going?"

I made a point of pulling my bike up alongside Taylor to make sure they didn't do anything to her. We both kept our eyes ahead of us. I kept watching that group of bikers ahead of us. We were getting closer to them and I was pretty sure one of them was my mom. Boy how I wanted my mom right now, and I especially wanted Taylor's grandfather. He'd know what to do. I could even use Jacques. The car was now moving closer to the two of us. I was getting worried they might try to knock into us or maybe even throw something at us to get us to crash.

"Beyonce, you want to go for a ride with us?" screamed the boy again and everyone inside the car started to laugh. "And is that your boy friend or some Frankenstein creature biking with you?" Again more laughter from inside.

I was about to say something when suddenly I heard a booming voice from behind yell out, "Boys, you better move that car on out of here."

I glanced behind me. It was Mr. Jacobs and his wife. They were biking fifteen or twenty yards behind us. Where the heck did they come from?

The two boys in the silver car started making kissing noises at me and Taylor. "So long, Beyonce. Maybe we'll see you later." And then the car sped off with them all making kissing noises.

Taylor and I stopped. We were both shaking a bit.

"Are you ok?" asked Mr. Jacobs' wife.

"I think so. Are you ok?" I tried to look into Taylor's eyes. We were both kind of shaken up

Taylor smiled. "Yes. Thanks for showing up when you did."

"We had stopped for a long lunch and I didn't get a good feeling about that car. I had seen them already yelling things out to other bikers," said Mr. Jacobs. "'Idiots. We also have them in Virginia."

"Don't tell my grandfather about this."

"What do you say, we all bike it in together," said Mr. Jacobs.

We were now passing road signs that read SARATOGA BATTLEFIELD, and one sign said it was only two miles away. None of us were talking. "Let's try and catch that group of four ahead of us," I said still kind of embarrassed about the Frankenstein insult.

It was a race. It was intense, and with about a mile to go to the battlefield, we finally came up alongside them.

"I knew you'd eventually catch us," said my mom. She was out of breath from the long steep hill we were climbing, and they were all glistening with sweat just like Taylor and me. We were so spent we couldn't even talk when we finally came upon them.

We stopped and pulled over off the road. It was great to finally stop biking. I even stepped out of my bike and leaned over to slow my breathing. I introduced Mr. Jacobs and his wife to the others. The two of them smiled and then they said they were going to continue biking.

Everyone wanted to know how our day had gone. Taylor and I looked at each other and basically went through all we had done except for the silver car, and even though it was nice to see the gang once again, I began to realize that my glorious day with her was over. The day had been mostly perfect, and it was something I'd never forget. Taylor had a boyfriend, a boyfriend who played soccer, and even that didn't matter anymore. Because I knew there was an electricity between us. I knew it and Taylor knew it.

As we turned left and biked up the steep Saratoga National Battlefield Road, I saw him before anyone else did, standing there at the entrance to the park, next to his bike.

My father was waving at us.

CHAPTER 10

When my mom saw my father she let out a soft groan and biked right up to him. The rest of us stopped our bikes about fifty yards away. That may not have been far enough.

"What are you doing here?" she said in a rather abrupt way.

Now I've never been the type to like confrontation, but my mom loves it. And Saratoga was about to get another battle. I saw all the signs as she got closer and closer to my dad: firm walk, firm jaw, one hand clenched, and a cool demeanor—icy, even—as she got ready to speak.

"I told you this morning not to show up here and bike the last stage."

My father just stood there with his arms out saying something but being drowned out by my mom.

"I take it this is your father," said Jacques.

I just nodded my head and wished I could evaporate.

My dad was still trying to speak to my mom, and then he saw me and waved. I gave him a weak wave back.

"It says here there will be buses beginning at 6:00 pm that will take us to some restaurant at Saratoga Lake." Murray was reading from his sweaty agenda as a distraction. It didn't work.

Taylor came alongside me. "Are you okay?"

"I am so embarrassed," I said stressing every word.

Taylor reached out and tapped me on my shoulder. "Hey, he loves you guys and must feel bad about not being here this week. Go say hi to him."

I slowly pedaled my bike over to the two of them. Other bikers moved around behind them trying to act busy, but they were listening to everything being said.

"Hi, Kevin."

"Hi, Dad."

"You had every chance to come on this trip," said my mother, her arms crossed over her chest. Her face was very red. "Even a day before we left I was still trying to get you to come. But not this way."

My dad looked around at the growing crowd of bikers staring at him. He was looking down at the ground like a little boy who had just eaten all the homemade cookies before dinner. "Jenny, please stop yelling. You're creating a scene."

"…and then when you called today and said you wanted to bike the last day, I said no, yet here you are anyway. That's disrespectful. It always has to be your way, Patrick, and I'm tired of it."

"So is this your husband, Jenny?" Jacques had come over to stand next to me.

My dad looked up and said hello to Jacques, who reached out to shake hands with him. "My name's Jacques Fortier. I'm from Ottawa."

My dad took his hand. "Nice to meet you. Patrick Walsh."

"You have a nice son here. He's a good boy, and your wife, well, she's just amazing. I took a bad fall yesterday, and she's taken good care of me. Helped get me to the doctor. She made me take my medicine. Helped me get back biking."

"And she changed my flat," said Murray, who also joined us.

"Yes, she is amazing," said my dad, and he smiled.

My mom still looked very angry, and I thought she was about to storm off somewhere.

"And, Jenny, isn't it nice that your husband cared so much about you and Kevin here that he wants to ride in the last day with you." Jacques looked directly at my mom, who just stared back, and then he turned and looked at my dad. "A year ago, I hit rock bottom. I was very depressed. I won't go into all the reasons why, but Murray here has been my rock." He pointed at Murray and placed his right arm on Murray's shoulder. "His love has helped me get through my struggles, and I'm not sure if I've ever actually thanked him for all he did and has continued to do for me. I'm a good one for cracking jokes and keeping everything light and jovial." We all kind of smiled when he said that. "But I'm not so good at telling the people I love how important they are to me." I could see Murray wiping a tear from his eye. "Well, I think Patrick here is showing the two of you how much he loves you."

I couldn't believe Jacques was saying such a thing.

My mom forced a smile, and her eyes looked a little moist. "But I told you how important it is for us to finish this ride together. You can't just show up on the last day."

My dad put his hand up to stop her. "All right. I'm sorry I did this. Standing here today and watching all the bikers come in has shown me how much this was a team effort; how much all of you bonded together. I can see I'm not a part of that, and I wish I had been. I'll put my bike back in the car. You were very clear this morning, and I still came. That was wrong."

"I'm sure he can come to dinner with us. It might be good to hear other stories." Murray said, holding his soggy agenda sheet. "It says here…"

My mom clenched her mouth shut, and gave Murray a nasty look. Murray knew enough to shut up. My mother was turning things around in her mind, trying to figure out what to say. "Would you like to come to dinner?"

My dad grinned. "I'd love it."

Before we left for dinner, my dad helped us set up our tents. He was a big help with Jacques, who was in a lot of pain after the day of biking and not good for much except sitting around and groaning. Dad sat around and listened to all our stories from the week as we went back and forth to the shower trucks.

The buses took us to a restaurant on the lakeshore that had indoor and outdoor seating. The food was good—way better than the dinners we had been getting this week and we had a lot of laughs. Some guy on the outdoor patio played Revolutionary War songs since we were camping that night at the battlefield. I never realized there were so many Revolutionary War songs. I introduced my dad to my Virginia friend and explained how we had biked together one day, and that he had run a bunch of Boston Marathons. "He even ran the day of the Boston Marathon bombing," I said.

My dad must be a good lawyer because he's always been very good at gathering information, talking, and meeting people. By the end of the meal, it seemed like he knew everyone on the ride. It occurred to me that if he had come along on this trip, the atmosphere would have been quite a bit different.

When the bus dropped us off at the battlefield, my dad said goodbye to everyone, shaking hands with ten or twelve people like a politician at a campaign rally, but he saved Jacques for last. "Thanks for what you said today. You're lucky to have Murray."

Jacques shrugged. "I'm not so sure he'd agree with you."

My mom and I walked with him to his car. "I'm still angry with you," she said.

He nodded. "I'm angry I didn't come along on day one, but I'll be there tomorrow to see you finish. I'm proud of you." And he looked at the two of us.

"It's not such a big deal," I said.

"It's a pretty big deal," said Mom. "Lake Placid to Albany, five days, over 200 miles, up and down hills—that's pretty big."

"Yeah, I guess."

"And you know what else is big? This is your last year to make states." She then turned to my father and made another point. Maybe demand is more like it. "You should come and see your son run more often."

"I will." Mom raised an eyebrow. Sometimes that's all it takes. "I will, I promise."

And we all hugged before he got in the car to

drive away. It wasn't the best hug I've ever seen between my parents, but it would still be classified as a hug.

"Do you think he'll really be at the Corning Preserve tomorrow?" I asked.

"He better be."

The Saratoga Battlefield was the darkest place we camped. The place is virtually unchanged from when the major Revolutionary War battle was fought here in 1777. This was where Benedict Arnold made a name for himself as a great military leader who helped defeat the British. Winning this battle turned the tide of that war and allowed France to come in and help us. If we had lost that battle, I would probably be speaking with an English accent right now, which is kind of a shame because I would actually like it if I had an English accent.

Before going to sleep, Taylor and I took a trail down a hill to a field that overlooked much of the battlefield. The moon cast a sort of milky shadow on everything. Above us we could see tent city and a few flashlights. We sat together on the damp ground and looked out over a peaceful area where, at one time, hundreds of people had been injured and killed.

"Not only don't I have a car, but I also don't have my license."

Taylor smiled. "I knew it. By the way, I liked your dad."

I could feel a sadness creeping into my body and moving up into my lungs and my throat. This would probably be my last night together with her. Tomorrow, we'd finish this ride and get back into our regular lives. Maybe I'd see her at a track or cross country meet. We'd say hello, but the magic would be gone.

"Yeah, he's a good guy, but he tries to please too many people. Too many of the wrong people."

"That was nice that he wanted to bike in with us on the last day. It was also nice when you moved your bike next to me when the jerks in the car were yelling. You wanted to protect me. I noticed that, and you don't look anything like Frankenstein."

I laughed, and we both just sat there. "I'm gonna really miss you." My voice was cracked a bit when I said this, but at least I didn't let out a gasp.

"I'm gonna miss you, too." Taylor then leaned into me, and I held her there. It was dark, but I'm pretty sure we both had tears coming down our face. I know I did.

Sometimes words are inadequate. There were no words to describe how I felt sitting there that night under a full moon high above that cast long shadows upon that historic battlefield. Fifteen minutes, thirty minutes, maybe an hour went by as we sat there embracing each other far more deeply than my parents did that evening. When I finally looked down at her and she looked up, our lips came together, and I finally understood why a kiss is one of the most sacred things we humans do—and I didn't need Google to show me how to do it.

CHAPTER 11

DAY 5: SARATOGA BATTLEFIELD
TO ALBANY CORNING PRESERVE 27 MILES

We were all sad as we took down our tents that final day. Even the sky looked sad. It was gray and overcast, and threatened rain since sun up. Mr. Jacobs, in the far distance, came firmly out of his tent with the battlefield behind him, and he really did look like someone about to launch an attack against the Yankees, except this general wore tight-fitting biker shorts.

At dinner the night before, Al gave a brief talk explaining that our breakfast would be on land once owned by General Peter Schuyler, seven miles from the battlefield in a little town on the Hudson River named Stillwater. Apparently, General Schuyler served in the

French and Indian War, and then as a general for the Continental Army in the Revolutionary War. After the war, he became a U.S. senator.

"He owned enslaved people," grumbled Taylor.

"And so did Jefferson and Washington," said her grandfather shaking his head.

"I never could understand why some of the most brilliant thinkers like Jefferson could own people," said my mom.

"Taylor and I were planning on skipping the breakfast at the Schuyler Mansion," said her grandfather.

I looked at her in a panic.

"But we talked about it and we've decided to go," said Taylor. "We're going because we want to spend the morning with you, not to honor him."

And that's when Taylor's grandfather cleared his throat and then recited a poem clearly with perfect pitch like he was a radio announcer.

> "I am the darker brother.
> They send me to eat in the kitchen
> When company comes,
> But I laugh,
> And eat well,
> And grow strong.
>
> Tomorrow,
> I'll be at the table
> When company comes.

Nobody'll dare
Say to me,
"Eat in the kitchen,"
Then.

Besides,
They'll see how beautiful I am
And be ashamed—

I, too, am America."

We all cheered and clapped our hands.

"Langston Hughes," said Taylor's grandfather. "One of my favorite poets."

"Very inspirational, but we're gonna have to bike seven miles to eat breakfast," said Jacques with his arms out in appeal.

"That's right," said Murray, "and then we have to eat on the property of a slave owner that brought about the deaths of hundreds, maybe even thousands, of my British ancestors."

"God bless America," my father began singing, as a few other bikers, and even Taylor's grandfather, joined in.

"Oh, Canada," Jacques and Murray each began singing, and we all began laughing.

It was fun and it was funny, but now it was the next morning, and seven miles seemed pretty far to bike to get something to eat. We were a bit depressed as we put our tents away in our bags for the last time and brought them to the trucks. Our sullen mood was finally broken by Taylor's grandfather. "Hey, what's going on here?"

We all looked at him and shrugged.

"We've biked almost 200 miles in four days, and today we're finishing," I said.

We still weren't smiling much.

"We're gonna see it through. We're gonna land this plane," said Taylor's grandfather.

"We have nothing to fear but fear itself," said Murray, and now we began laughing.

"We have met the enemy and he is us," said Jacques. Now we started clapping our hands.

"Ask not what your country can do for you, but what you can do for your country," said my mom. And then everyone laughed and looked at me

"Long may you run. Although these changes have come, long may you run." It was the first thing that jumped into my head. "It's my favorite Neil Young song." And now we turned to Taylor.

She stood there thinking. You could almost see her mind working, going through, trying to find an acceptable quote. "Are we gonna get busy living, or get busy dying?" We all just stared at her. "That's a line from my favorite movie, *The Shawshank Redemption*."

We all let out a cheer and Taylor's grandfather screamed, "Let's get busy living!"

The seven-mile ride was mostly downhill to Route 4, and when we finally got to the Schuyler Mansion, we were impressed with not only how beautiful the house and the grounds were, but how the biking organization had put up a few tents with tables and chairs and were serving all sorts of breakfast foods, from bagels to yogurt and pancakes.

"They've really done a great job on this trip," said Taylor's grandfather, and he made a point of seeking out Al and a few of his co-workers to thank them for such a great five days. He also said he wanted to see where the slave quarters were and if any of them had been buried on the grounds.

I sat next to Taylor, and we huddled together since it was a bit breezy and chilly. It occurred to me that this might be the last time I'd ever get to sit next to her. I didn't have much of an appetite, but I forced down one pancake and tried to laugh at some of the lame jokes told by Murray and Jacques. My mom sat next to Jacques, looking about as sad as I must have looked.

It would be a short day. We only had another eighteen or twenty miles to go for the finish. I could literally count down the hours I had left with Taylor.

"I wonder what the finish is gonna be like?" my mom asked.

"Well, I've been on a few bike trips before," said Murray. "Usually, you just bike under a canopy of balloons, and everyone takes a picture, and that's it. It's rather anti-climactic, given everything that leads up to it."

"I heard your president might be there to greet us," said Jacques.

We all groaned.

As this talk went on, Taylor reached out with her right hand and took hold of my left hand. I held her hand and concentrated on how wonderful and soft and warm it felt. I wanted to remember her touch forever. We didn't hide that we were holding hands, and I wanted to stand up and cry out that it wasn't fair that we had to finish today. I wanted to live the rest of my life in my tent and bike fifty miles every day and eat lunch and breakfast with everyone at that table and sit out in the dark every night and hold Taylor and kiss her.

"Do you want more OJ?" My mom was standing up, but looking at me, and noticing that I was holding Taylor's hand.

I shook my head no.

As we continued the ride, the wind seemed to pick up down by the river, and it was mostly in our faces. I wasn't enjoying the ride along Route 4—not with all the cars and the potholes—but I knew when we got to Cohoes, we'd soon be on the bike trail. We weren't talking much, and because of Jacques, our pace was very slow. We kept hearing a lot of "On your left," as bikers zoomed by us. Why were so many of those bikers in a good mood?

When we finally reached the bike trail, it was smooth and wide, allowing us to once again bike in pairs. The Hudson River rolled along on our left, and tall trees on both sides of the trail surrounded us. It was a perfect way to conclude our five-day ride.

Occasionally, we'd catch a few glimpses of the city of Albany, with its tall buildings, directly in front of us. "I think we have about a mile to go," said Murray after a quick glance at his odometer.

"Let's stop for a second," said my mom, and we all pulled off the trail and onto the grass on the right. We stood there quietly as my mom looked at each of us. "I don't know what that finish is going to be like, but before we get there I just want to say thank you. This was wonderful."

We all looked to the ground and nodded our heads and she continued. "I wanted to do this with my son, and I ended up making four dear friends along the way. I never expected that."

There were a few acknowledgements from us about how we had become good friends in only a few days. My mom then looked at Taylor. "You have had a terrible thing happen to you, but how blessed you are to have such a wonderful grandfather. That's real love over there."

We were all sniffling now as she turned and looked right at Murray. "And here's another example of love, this guy, who takes his depressed partner along on a bike trip to cheer him up." We all nodded our approval, and Taylor's grandfather reached out and patted Murray on the shoulder.

"It was working up till this moment," said Jacques, and he had two tears streaking down his face. "Anyone have a Kleenex?"

Four of us dug deep into our bike bags to give him a Kleenex.

My mom now looked at Jacques. "You kept us laughing, but we all know you're not laughing so much inside, are you?" He shrugged. "Anyone who can see and notice others the way you can will never be down for long. And how fortunate to have found the right person." We all smiled and looked at Murray.

She slowly turned in my direction. "And then there's my wonderful seventeen-year-old son who came on a five-day biking trip with his mother. Can you believe that—with his mother?" And we all sort of chuckled. "You didn't have to do that. The one thing I learned on this trip is how lucky I am to have a son like you."

She put her two hands out, and we all began holding hands until it became a group hug. It probably looked pretty corny to the other bikers rolling past, but we didn't care. We were all sort of sniffling as we got back on our bikes and pedaled toward the Corning Preserve and the finish line.

・

As we came out from under a canopy of trees, we could see a lot of activity ahead of us. A high-school band was playing marching music just beyond an enormous banner saying WELCOME ADIRONDACK BIKERS. The last one hundred yards were partitioned off with an array of balloons and flags, and all sorts of people stood behind police barriers applauding for us as we rode through.

"Well, I never expected this," said Murray with a big grin on his face as we rode under the banner.

"Taylor! Taylor!" There was a black high school guy standing just beyond the finish line to the side of the banner with a bouquet of roses.

Taylor smiled and waved to him. "Hi, Drew!" She got off her bike and he gave her a big hug, his two strong arms completely enveloping her.

I had to look away. That's when I noticed my mom scanning the crowd. "Where's your father?"

I looked all around, but it was just a sea of unfamiliar faces. No one who knew us came to see our finish. Not Dwight, not Dipper, not even a distant relative, and certainly not my father. Why would anyone come to see me finish one of the biggest events of my life? Holding back what I had left of tears, I walked away, leaving Taylor to Drew and my mom to her silence and anger and disappointment that my dad had not come as promised.

Pushing my bike forward, hoping to be swallowed by the same sea of unfamiliar faces, I looked up toward the pedestrian bridge that takes you into downtown Albany. I was the first to see him. He was dodging through foot traffic coming down the last leg of the bridge.

My dad was running toward us.

"Here he comes!" I yelled.

When he finally got to us, I could tell my mom wasn't too happy.

"I've been waiting here for an hour, and then I got an email that something came up at the courthouse. I was only gone for about fifteen minutes." He was out of breath. "I can't believe I missed you. Can the two of you bike back out so I can get a picture of you finishing?"

"We're not gonna do that," said my mom.

"Do it," said Jacques.

She gave him a sort of nasty look, but my mom and I, under protest, walked our bikes down, and when we had a chance, moved them under the barrier to bike back to the finish so he could take a picture of us. "If he's a changed man," said my mom quietly to me, "he's not getting off to a good start."

"But it is a start," I said, defending him.

As we rode through the finish a second time I could see Taylor introducing her boyfriend to Murray and Jacques.

"Hey, Lance Armstrong, give us a smile."

I looked to my left and there was the Dipper holding his cell phone and getting a picture of me. He stood there with another runner friend, Ryan. "We were at McDonald's in Delmar," said Dipper, "and then I remembered you were finishing today, so we looked for this preserve place. It was hard to find, so we just got here. Smile."

I gave him a thumbs up, and even my mom smiled. "That's so nice your friends came."

"Yeah, it is," I said. I liked the sound of that, *my friends,* and I thought about bringing them over to meet Taylor, who was off standing on the grass next to her bike and beaming with both hands around her bouquet of roses, which are the flowers of love, flowers that I had not bought for her, flowers that were bought by her boyfriend Drew.

CHAPTER 12

My dad wanted to take us out to lunch at some place in Albany. "After we eat, I'll drive you over to the train station where you can pick up your car. Do you want to invite your friends?"

Jacques and Murray said they needed to make their long drive back to Ottawa, and Taylor, her grandfather, and her boyfriend had already made plans to eat at some other place in Troy. Dipper and Ryan were all charged up about coming to eat, though.

"I'll see you at the meets," I said to Taylor. We stared at each other. She held Drew's hand just like she had held mine earlier in the day at breakfast. He, however, was looking at his watch like he needed to get somewhere. "And, Drew, that was nice of you to bring Taylor flowers."

"Thanks. Nice to meet you."

I looked Drew right in the eyes. "Taylor and I biked together a lot this week. She's amazing. She got me through some long biking days."

Drew smiled. "She is amazing."

And then I began walking away with Dipper and Ryan to rejoin my parents.

"Hey, she's a babe," said Dipper.

I didn't get too far when I felt a tap on my shoulder. "Here, take one." Taylor gave me one of the long-stem roses from the bouquet, then gave me one of those brother-sister hugs.

I put that rose in a mug of water on my dresser, and it sits there still today almost two months later. It doesn't look too pretty anymore, but I just can't throw it away. A week or so after the trip, I watched *The Shawshank Redemption* on Netflix. I had never seen it before, but now I understood why it was Taylor's favorite. It's about hope and never giving up, two qualities that describe her perfectly.

Taylor and I became Facebook and Instagram friends, and for the first few weeks after the trip she called and texted me quite a bit. She sent me pictures from our ride, and we had a lot of laughs talking about the trip. The picture of us lying on the beach at Lake George was something I looked at every day, though lately I've only looked at it once a week or so. I also saw some of what she was doing on Facebook—her trips with Drew to Saratoga, and the times they went to the movies, and soon it was the first day of cross-country practice. As my life got busy, that bike trip seemed like it happened years ago.

I was running well, more content to sit behind Dwight and pace off him at practice. He had recovered quickly from his ankle injury, and the local paper referred to us as the best 1-2 punch in the area. Dwight always got the most press and the most attention in school, and people were always hanging out by his locker. Teachers called him "Mr. Track Star" in class.

Our first meet was a big invitational in early September at my favorite course: Saratoga Spa State Park. All the top area teams would be there, and it would be the first time I'd see Taylor in person since early July. Was I more excited about the race or about seeing Taylor? I wasn't sure, but when our bus pulled into the parking lot that day, all I kept doing was looking for the blue uniforms of Holy Family.

Even my parents were going that day. My dad was trying to spend more time with us. He came home earlier most nights, and did not check his work email as much from home. He and mom also had a few dates, trips to the movies, and even dinner a couple of times. I have no idea if they're going to make it and what will happen with them when I go to college. My mom is busy back teaching, but every now and then I've caught her a few times reading something on her cell phone before taking a Kleenex to blow her nose. When I look at her she'll say something like, "My allergies this year are the worst I can remember."

But today was my day—our first cross-country invitational—and at this meet the varsity boys ran first. I looked for Taylor while I jogged and warmed up on the course. I knew she'd be out there. She had texted me the night before and told me she was running varsity and wanted to wish me good luck. Her race went off about an hour after mine, so maybe she'd be on the course when I ran by. I was nervous for that first race, and if I could just see her, maybe that would calm me down a bit. She always gave me courage, like the time I jumped off that rock in Blue Mountain Lake. I think that was her greatest gift to me.

I'm not sure if anyone on my team could sense I was a different runner, but I knew it, and I think my coach knew it, too. I had more confidence. You see, I was no longer running to get away from something, like teachers and bullies and my parents. I was now running to get somewhere. That little shift in my attitude made me more relaxed, and I loved running for all the right reasons. Now, I knew I was doing something I had been created to do. It wasn't about how fast I ran or who I beat. It was about capturing that feeling when everything is working together just perfectly.

Maybe Dwight had noticed the difference. In workouts he was going flat-out and breathing heavily, while I was right there smoothly moving just behind him. You never heard one exaggerated breath out of me. I didn't mind that he set the pace—I shadowed him the whole way.

The seven of us on varsity lined up in box ten. There were over one hundred other runners standing behind the white starting line, waiting for the gun. We huddled together as a team and gave our usual cheer and slapped hands. Dwight looked me in the eye and said, "Good luck, Kevin." Just before a race was usually the only time he ever really spoke or acknowledged me.

I said the same back knowing that, on that day, I didn't need luck.

When the gun went off, we raced the 600-meter straightaway before turning right and making a sharp left turn down a steep pebbly hill. As usual, Dwight was in the lead, and I was about fifteenth in the closely packed group of runners. Last year, I may have panicked to be this far back, but not this year. This year I had faith in my ability. This year I knew there was a beautiful girl at this meet who kissed me on an equally beautiful night in early July, and I knew she loved me even if we'd never be together. Just knowing that was enough. I began to move by runners one after another.

I was focused completely on the race, but was still aware of the spectators. I could hear Dipper's screaming and encouragement at his usual place in the back woods, but where was Holy Family? Was their bus late? Did they decide not to come?

At the first mile, I was in tenth place. I could count all the runners ahead of me. Some of them seemed to be slowing down, but not Dwight. He charged ahead with each stride. He looked much stronger than he had looked at practice. A few doubts crept in. Maybe he was now totally recovered from his ankle injury and finally running at the top of his ability? If that was true, then he deserved to beat me. I wasn't necessarily in this race to beat Dwight. What I was after was that feeling, that feeling of fulfilling my destiny to run this 3.1-mile race to the best of my ability, to do what I had been made to do.

We ran around the Saratoga Park Pool. I passed a few more runners. Dwight seemed to be getting further away. He was now all by himself. We then ran downhill on another gravel trail. *You've got plenty of time*, I told myself. *Just open up the stride with your long legs and let them do the work.* It felt great to run this fast and this relaxed as I passed a few more runners.

"You and Dwight are kickin' butt," screamed the Dipper. "Keep it right there, and we're gonna win this meet." I always loved how that guy would move all around the course to encourage us.

And now the long uphill, the make or break part of the course that all runners refer to as 'Fern Gully,' a 200-meter winding uphill stretch to the two-mile mark. I was in third place. Dwight pumped his arms twenty, maybe thirty yards ahead of me and that's when I heard all the cheering. It was Dwight's fan club—his girlfriend and all her friends—maybe ten in all. They jumped up and down and screamed his name, just like they did at every meet. They were always at the two-mile mark at Saratoga, and I should have expected that, but still, it sort of hit me like a punch to my stomach. I heard a few non-emotional "Go, Kevin's" when I ran by, but most of his fan club were already on the move to the finish line to see Dwight win this first invitational of the season.

At the top of Fern Gully stood my coach, who screamed and cheered for both of us. "We're gonna win this, guys. Work together! Finish strong!"

I was now alongside the second place runner, still twenty or so yards behind Dwight. We turned left, back into the woods, for about a half-mile. We would emerge at the end for the quick 600-meter sprint to the finish line.

I gauged my body. Feet feel okay. Legs strong. Arms pumping well in easy rhythm. Head relaxed and not bobbing from side-to-side. No problems--except Dwight. He was the only runner ahead of me as we went in to the darkest part of the woods and the most remote section of the course. I could see some movement ahead of me, which was odd, because there were usually no spectators or other runners back here. Was Dwight slowing down? I seemed to be getting closer with each stride.

I heard them before I saw them. It was Taylor and seven of her teammates. They were all screaming my name. Each of them held a white poster about two feet by two feet, and each poster had one word with dark black lettering on it. The girls all stood in an organized row so that you had to read one word at a time, and they screamed and yelled my name in unison. The posters, when all strung together, said **KEVIN GET BUSY LIVING OR GET BUSY DYING.**

I could feel the hair stand up on the back of my head. I know I smiled even though I was tired and had already run over two miles up and down hills. I was in second place while running faster on this course than I had ever run. I was most definitely living.

But did I have enough life left in me to win this race?

A hundred yards ahead of us the trees ended, and we raced the last 600 meters across a flat field. It was like we were coming from the dark and into the light. Groups of runners and a few parents and coaches stood in the light looking down the trail to see the top finishers. Dwight had gone into the woods with a comfortable lead, but here was some other runner stride for stride next to him. When I pulled even with Dwight I could sense his shoulders sag a bit. He knew what I knew. He knew this race on this day belonged to me. He had given it his all. He had gone out hard. He had raced, but he couldn't shake me on this day.

Should I go by Dwight now while I was still in the woods, or should I wait till we came out into the sun? I admired how hard he had raced, and as I went by him, I wanted to shout something to the world and to Dwight and to all the people who once took me for granted, but that would be poor sportsmanship. I wanted to yell "On your left," but I didn't. I ran to the finish feeling perfect on this day, like a Beethoven symphony, like a van Gogh painting, and I watched the shocked, wide-eyed, open-mouthed expressions of all the people lining those last 600 meters who had expected Dwight to win.

AFTERWORD

I'd like to thank Kim Michelle O'Neal, for giving my book an early read and Roxanne Wegman for allowing me to use the amazing photo on the cover of the book. I was fortunate to have coached both Kim and Roxanne years ago, and I value their friendship. My wife Judy and my daughter Erin were also important readers for me, and I greatly valued their opinions.

The idea to write this book occurred to me as I was biking the annual Parks and Trails New York Cycle the Erie Canal from Buffalo to Albany in 2013 with over 400 other cyclists.

We met people from all over the country and from Canada. Most of us slept in tents every night usually covering entire athletic fields at various public high schools.

I biked with a group of people going at my pace, and just about every day I biked with a mom and her 17-year-old son. One day at a rest stop I struck up a conversation with them. They were both from Canada. The mom was a teacher, and the boy played soccer.

After that conversation I got back on my bike and began thinking there was no way I would ever have gone on an eight day bike trip with my mom when I was 17. With so much time on the bike I began to think through a story of a teenage boy biking with his mom in a group ride. Why is he doing this? What kind of kid was he? Where is the father? Is there a father? What if he met a girl his age on the ride and fell in love with her?

Every day after that I looked forward to getting back on the bike so I could return to this story I was creating. I desperately wanted to find out what was going to happen. As I began to create the 17-year old boy in my imagination, I also thought of my college friend Tom Meagher who I used to run with. He was a bit awkward and was much taller than me, but he was also one of the kindest and most sensitive people I ever met. Tom died far too many years ago, but as I wrote this story he came alive again for me.